A CHRISTIAN GUIDE
TO THE CLASSICS

Other Christian Guides to the Classics

Augustine's "Confessions"

Bunyan's "The Pilgrim's Progress"

The Devotional Poetry of Donne, Herbert, and Milton

Dickens's "Great Expectations"

Hawthorne's "The Scarlet Letter"

Homer's "The Odyssey"

Milton's "Paradise Lost"

Shakespeare's "Hamlet"

Shakespeare's "Macbeth"

A CHRISTIAN GUIDE TO THE CLASSICS

LELAND RYKEN

CROSSWAY®

WHEATON, ILLINOIS

Trade paperback ISBN: 978-1-4335-4703-4
ePub ISBN: 978-1-4335-4706-5
PDF ISBN: 978-1-4335-4704-1
Mobipocket ISBN: 978-1-4335-4705-8

Library of Congress Cataloging-in-Publication Data

Ryken, Leland.
  A Christian guide to the classics / Leland Ryken.
    pages cm.— (Christian guides to the classics)
  ISBN 978-1-4335-4703-4 (tp)
  1. Christianity and literature. I. Title.
PN49.R885   2015
809—dc23   2015003666

Crossway is a publishing ministry of Good News Publishers.

Contents

Preface

This book is a defense of works of literature (and by implication works of art and music and even nonartistic texts like political and historical ones) that go by the name of *classic*. In our current cultural situation, several distinct groups exist in relation to the classics. One is enlightened non-Christians who value the classics in many of the same ways that Christians value them. A second group is people of liberal (or "politically correct") persuasion who have a knee-jerk negative reaction to the classics and try to eliminate them from the public's possession and school curricula. A third group is Christians who value the classics.

In this book, all supporters of the classics, Christians and non-Christians alike, would agree with most of what I say in defense of the classics. We will see, however, that a Christian worldview and outlook supply a few additional arguments and lines of defense. This is why the book is entitled *A Christian Guide to the Classics*. Christians have a value-added defense of the classics and methodology for assimilating them.

Every art form, discipline of thought, and activity (such as sports) has its classics. In this book, I have discussed the subject in terms of literature because I am a literary scholar, and additionally because this book belongs to a Crossway series of Christian guides to literary classics. Nevertheless, what I say about literary classics has ready carryover to other art forms and disciplines.

To defend the classics requires that we understand what they are. The lay of the land for this book consists of answering three main questions, spread over multiple chapters:

1. What is a classic?
2. Of what value is a classic?
3. How should we read and assimilate a classic?

CHAPTER 1

Misconceptions about the Classics

There have always been misconceptions about the classics, but until recently these were relatively minor. The picture changed when liberal or "politically correct" advocates wrongly decided that the classics are harmful to society. These false claims need to be refuted. We need to realize at the outset of our discussion that all claims made about the classics are self-revealing of the people who make the claims. The rival positions often say less about the classics themselves and say more about the values and mind-sets of the people who hold the positions. The Christian defense of the classics grows out of the Christian value structure, and attacks on the classics are rooted in the worldview and political outlook of the attackers.

I will note in advance that some of the material covered in this chapter will be taken up in greater detail at various points later in this book.

The context in which any defense of the classics occurs today is the contemporary assault on the classics by people of liberal persuasion. They are the ones who have made the classics a life-or-death matter intellectually and educationally by attempting to suppress the classics and keep people from reading them.

Misconception #1: *The classics are irrelevant to us today because they come to us from long ago.*

This claim of irrelevance is an expression of what some scholars call "the myth of the contemporary." Those who hold this mind-set think everything contemporary is automatically better than what preceded it. Correspondingly, something that belongs to the past is inferior. Sometimes this expands into a presumptive rejection of everything from the past for no better reason than that it comes from the past.

The first thing to say is that this viewpoint presupposes that the past holds little value for us today. The issue of how we should regard the past will loom large in later sections of this book, so we do not need to say a lot about it here. At this early point, all we need to do is express disagreement with the premise that the past is irrelevant. Under that umbrella, we can note the following:

One way in which the liberal establishment has killed the classics is to remove them from course syllabi. About thirty years ago professors and students in English departments started to lose interest in literature and to replace it with other material. A graduate student is recorded as saying that he was bored with Wordsworth's poetry but couldn't get enough of the philosopher Heidegger. The result is that in most English courses today, literary texts are barely touched.

- Anyone who looks at the contemporary scene can see that it does not represent an ideal. On many fronts the modern world is in a state of decline. To hold it up as an ideal by which to denigrate the past is preposterous. At the very least, we need to be open to the possibility that taking an excursion into the accumulated wisdom of the past by way of the classics might provide an avenue for bringing order to our present situation.
- The pleasure principle is also a relevant consideration. For people who develop the capacity to enjoy being transported from their own time and place to a world of long ago, reading the classics is one of the inexpensive pleasures of life. It is a right and a delight that we can exercise simply by opening a book.
- The classics have a particular knack for capturing what is universal in human experience. As a result, they are perpetually up-to-date, contrary to what devotees of the contemporary myth claim. The case can be made that Homer is as up-to-date and relevant as a contemporary novel. It just takes more interpretive skill to see the relevance of Homer,

and that is where literature courses and published literary criticism show their worth.

- Taking excursions into the past by reading the classics opens up alternatives to the way things are in our everyday world. At every point in history, good alternatives have existed to the current situation regardless of what ultimately occurred. If we do not tap that source of insight, we become victims of what is imposed on us by the circumstances and thinking of the present.

The foregoing barely scratches the surface of what can be said about the benefits that come from the classics by virtue of their pastness; more will be said in later chapters.

Something additional that needs to be noted is that not all classics come to us from the past. Many of the classics of the past were originally classics in their own time. There have always been contemporary classics. Even if we decide that a classic needs to stand the test of time before fully meeting the criteria of becoming a classic, the passage of time merely validates the status of the work as being a classic. It had the qualities that made it a classic right from the start.

Misconception #2: *The classics are elitist and instruments of social oppression.*

This line of thought requires some unpacking. We can start with the charge of elitism. There are multiple fallacies in the claim that the classics are elitist, but also some truth. We can start with the obvious: to enjoy reading the classics, we need to be initiated into them. Until we are introduced to

"Nowhere has the attack on the old literature been more strident than in the very place where we might have expected that it would have been most stoutly defended, the university literary departments. . . . The activities of [those] who have been taking the old literature apart seem oftentimes so excessively violent, so irrational, and so counter-productive, so contrary to self-interest as to mystify us" (Alvin Kernan, "What Killed Literature").

Homer or Milton or Hawthorne, they are a foreign world to us. The corresponding question is, "So what?" This is true of every human activity or skill or realm of thought.

We do not know how to write until we are taught to do so. Until we learn to read, we are excluded from reading books. We cannot play baseball until we are initiated into the rules of the game and the techniques of holding a bat and throwing the ball. Playing the piano requires us to take piano lessons as a prerequisite. There is nothing elitist about any of these activities. It is simply in the nature of life that we are prevented from doing certain things until we are initiated into them, usually by someone who takes us under wing and educates us. The word *elitist* carries automatic sinister overtones that need to be rejected.

The charge of elitism usually implies that someone is acting as a gatekeeper to keep people on the outside from entering. But reading the classics does not exclude anyone. Classic books are free in a library or can be found inexpensively at hand. The only force of exclusion from the classics is the inertia or unawareness of the person who has not yet entered that world. The gateway to the classics is wide open for anyone to enter. All it takes to enter the "realms of gold" (John Keats's metaphor) that we know as the classics is to allow oneself to be educated into the joys of reading them.

There is a small way in which the claim of elitism is true. One dimension of being elite is that in whatever field, the pursuit of excellence—raising the bar of achievement high—does not appeal to most people. As a result, the people who value the best almost automatically place themselves into a

"Nor do I agree that great books and ideas are distinctively masculine; nor that they are at all elitist. On the contrary, I believe them to be distinctively human and eminently democratic. They have survived the ages precisely because they are accessible to people of different backgrounds and characters, all of whom can aspire to understand them and to be elevated by them" (Gertrude Himmelfarb, "Revolution in the Library").

smaller category. To those who are content with a lower level of achievement (or who have not been educated into something higher), a common maneuver is to stigmatize achievers with the label *elitism*. At this point we need to accept the label as honorific.

For example, anyone who strives to follow Jesus's command in the Sermon on the Mount that "you therefore must be perfect, as your heavenly Father is perfect" (Matt. 5:48) is in a small and "elite" group within the broader society. So much the better. We do not denounce all-American basketball players because only a few rise to that small circle of superior athletes, nor do we attempt to prevent the public from playing basketball. Instead we honor the small circle of players who rise to the top.

The claim that reading Homer's *Odyssey* or Toni Morrison's *Beloved* is an instrument of oppression should be named for what it is—preposterous. The classics as a whole embody the entire range of intellectual and political viewpoints that the human race has produced through the ages. They are not monolithic. At the heart of the "politically correct" enterprise is censorship. Attempting to keep people from reading the classics is in fact an instrument of suppression. We live in a cultural situation in which the liberal establishment attempts to deny people access to any literary work that does not advance the propagandistic cause of liberalism. There is absolutely no way in which reading Dickens's *Great Expectations* enslaves anyone who reads it. The censorship consists of the attempt to make sure that no one reads Dickens if certain people do not wish to read him.

Misconception #3: *Because we know that classics are great works, we can presume that they tell us the truth.*

The two misconceptions discussed above share the quality of undervaluing the classics. But it is also possible to overvalue them or value them incorrectly. This is a danger that resides with those who elevate the classics, just as the first two misconceptions belong to people who dislike the classics and attempt to make sure that people do not have access to them. It is possible to attach an automatic and arbitrary positive value to the classics that they do not entirely merit.

The most common manifestation of this is to venerate the classics (and especially those belonging to the classical Greco-Roman tradition) so highly that in effect they are regarded as being beyond criticism. No work of literature is above criticism. The fact that a classic is artistically and intellectually great does not necessarily mean that it embodies the truth. We know this partly because the classics do not agree among themselves. In fact, taken together, they express the full range of human thinking and feeling, both good and bad. Additionally, the only book that Christians should presuppose to be completely trustworthy and truthful is the Bible. We need to weigh *whether* all other works match up to biblical truth, not presume *that* they do.

The fact that a great artist portrays a world view "does not mean that we should automatically accept that world view. Art may heighten the impact of the world view (in fact, we can count on this), but it does not make something true" (Frances Schaeffer, *Art and the Bible*).

Misconception #4: *The classics are relics in the museum of the past, and their primary function is to preserve the past as something that we can visit.*

Earlier I made the case that part of the value of the classics is the very fact that most of them come to us from the past (and many of them from the *distant* past). But this line of defense, too, can be carried to an untenable extreme. Some enthusiasts for the classics view them only as a gateway to the past, with no regard to what is contemporary in them. These people are historians and antiquarians at heart; they simply like to know about past people and cultures.

There is nothing wrong with this love to know about the past. However, to read the classics only as giving us information about the past is to reduce the scope of what they stand ready to give us. In fact, that would be to make them a source of historical data instead of a living presence. Works of literature embody universal and timeless human experience, and the classics should be read as imparting that form of knowledge to us. The classics are partly windows to the past, but as works of literature they are (even more) pictures of what is true for all people at all times in all places, including us.

Misconception #5: *Classics are by definition long and difficult works.*

We most readily think of the classics in terms of masterworks—long works such as epics and novels and perhaps, with a little bending of the definition, plays such as those of Shakespeare. These works are difficult and demanding, requiring literary expertise and sophistication. They are works that are studied in advanced high school courses and college literature courses.

Several things are wrong with this automatic assumption that classics are necessarily long masterworks.

First, every genre has its classics, including

"There are various legitimate reasons for teaching a diversity of works in college classrooms, but at the heart of our curriculum should be the 'canon'—a list of classic works that embody in a universally significant manner the common experience of men and women and enable us, by studying them, to grow into the full humanity that we share with others. . . . We teach such works because they help us to discern the order and purpose in human existence. . . . An acquaintance with great literature is certainly no substitute for character, but it enhances the moral imagination and is a good thing in itself" (R. V. Young, *At War with the Word*).

short works and simple ones. There are classic nursery rhymes (Mother Goose) and children's literature (*The Tale of Peter Rabbit*). Dick and Jane is a classic first-grade reader. There are classic riddles and sayings ("A penny for your thoughts"). There are classic hymns ("Amazing Grace") and proverbs ("Curiosity killed the cat"). Folk stories, such as Little Red Riding Hood or Paul Bunyan, can be classics. So can murder mysteries (Sherlock Holmes). I offer these categories simply as examples that show that a classic does not need to be a long and difficult masterwork.

Second, short lyric poems can be classics. Hundreds of them are. They meet all the criteria that will be explored in chapter 2. It is therefore misleading to picture the classics, either to ourselves or others, as being more formidable than they are.

Furthermore, we are all entitled to have our own private list of classics. If they serve the function of classics in our personal lives, they are classics to us. The Narnia books by C. S. Lewis and the Little House books by Laura Ingalls Wilder have been classics to generations of families. They are children's books for children and also adult books for adults, and in both cases they are simple stories and not epics on a par with Milton's *Paradise Lost*.

Finally, the Bible is the supreme classic. Is it a masterwork? Yes, but that is not how Christians through the centuries have experienced it. They have experienced it as an everyday companion in their lives. The Bible has been the most accessible of all books for believing families and individuals. If the Bible is a classic, all Christians have at least one great classic in their repertoire. If they have one, they can have many.

Frederick Buechner is a sophisticated literary and theological writer. Yet he has many times claimed that L. Frank Baum's *The Wonderful Wizard of Oz* is one of the enduring and influential classics in his life. He claimed that *The Wonderful Wizard of Oz* is "not only the greatest fairy tale this nation has produced but one of its great myths" (*The Annotated Wizard of Oz*). Buechner said in an interview that he "lived in Oz more than in whatever house we were living in at the time." He even made *The Wonderful Wizard of Oz* the basis of one of his novels.

To value the classics does not require us to have an advanced literary education. This is not to disparage the classic masterworks. For people of sophisticated literary taste, they are the best of the best. What is most important, however, is to value classics in whatever form they enter our lives. Of course, to aspire to the highest is always a virtue. Additionally, all education is ultimately self-education. The way to acquire a taste for the classics is to read them. The tragedy would be to settle for our current level of attainment and not aim higher than that.

Chapter Summary

Before we construct a case for the classics and a methodology for reading them, we need to clear the ground of obstacles. Many of the obstacles come from people who try to keep the classics out of our schools and out of sight in our culture, but some of the wrong thinking about the classics also comes from their advocates. The positive antidotes to the fallacies explored in this chapter are the following:

- The classics are important to us today, partly because they are a voice from the past and partly because they speak to the universal human condition.
- The classics do not enslave anyone and in fact liberate those who read them (in ways to be explored later).
- But the classics are not infallible, with the result that they always need to be critiqued by Christian standards of truth and morality.
- Classics are available to us at whatever level of literary sophistication we possess;

"Full-scale revival will come only when English professors recommit themselves to slaking the human craving for contact with works of art that somehow register one's own longings and yet exceed what one has been able to articulate by and for oneself. This is among the indispensable experiences of the fulfilled life" (Andrew Delbanco, "The Decline and Fall of Literature").

"The humanities are an essentially human enterprise. . . . The record of that enterprise reposes in the library in the form of books. . . . These are the books that sustain our minds and inspire our imaginations. It is there that we look for truth, for knowledge, for wisdom" (Gertrude Himmelfarb, "Revolution in the Library").

if we cannot yet master a Shakespearean tragedy, we can read Tolkien's The Lord of the Rings.

What Is a Classic?

The first thing to say is that the concept of a classic is not limited to literature (although that is the subject of this book). Most objects and events in our lives have examples that rise to the status of being a classic. "Give the gift of a timeless classic," says an advertisement for a watch. "It's a classic," a wife tells her husband as they look at suits in a clothing store. In some American towns, residents can saunter downtown one evening per week during the summer to see displays of classic cars. One of the ESPN television channels is called ESPN Classic; it specializes in reruns of past sports events or profiles of athletes from the past. It is obvious, then, that when an English professor tells a prospective student and her parents that "we still teach the classics," the professor is tapping into something universal and not only literary.

A second preliminary observation is that the universal concept *classic* should not be confused with the adjective *classical*. Classical literature and art were produced by the ancient Greek and Roman civilizations. The classical school movement derives its inspiration and content from Greco-Roman civilization and is not necessarily built around classics from all eras. (It is also the case, though, that people who value classical edu-

The classics are a paradox. On the one hand, they are the best of the best and belong to a very elite circle of the very greatest works. They raise the bar high in terms of what they demand from us. On the other hand, many of them are familiar to us because they have traditionally been central in our educational experience. Some classics that we have not yet read are familiar to us by simple cultural osmosis. For example, even if we have not read Shakespeare's *Hamlet*, we probably know that Hamlet is a brooding loner who toys with a skull in a churchyard and utters a famous soliloquy that begins, "To be, or not to be: that is the question." Most people know about Hester's scarlet letter even before they read Hawthorne's great story about it.

cation in this specialized sense tend to embrace the classics generally, even when they are not ancient in origin.)

A third thing to note at the outset is that in popular culture today, words such as *classic* and *epic* are tossed around as honorific terms with little specific meaning—like the all-purpose adjective *awesome*. When people do this, the word *classic* is assumed to carry automatic positive associations and is little more than a way to express enthusiasm for the work or event in question. Often publishers resort to the quick fix of pinning the label *classic* on a book that they wish to promote. It was an editor who once changed a book title from *Reading Literature with C. S. Lewis* (the accurate title) to *Reading the Classics with C. S. Lewis* (a title that the marketing department thought would carry more popular appeal). As the author of multiple guides to the classics, I am of course gratified by this vote of confidence for the classics, but it is important that we validate the label with some genuine content.

> There are many famous essays and books that address the question of what makes a classic. T. S. Eliot wrote an essay "What Is a Classic?" and his statement on historical longevity is often quoted: "It is only by hindsight, and in historical perspective, that a classic can be known as such."

Toward a Definition of the Term *Classic*

Every academic discipline, as well as such cultural pursuits as sports and cooking, has its classics. That is useful to keep in mind as we consider the concept of a literary classic. It helps to think of a literary classic in light of classics in other spheres because the literary definitions that I am about to quote can illuminate the concepts of a sports classic or a classic family photograph as well.

The format that I have chosen for this chapter is to quote some touchstone definitions of a literary classic and then unpack what these complementary definitions tell us. Here are the definitions:

- "We speak of a book as a classic when it has gained a place for itself in our culture, and has consequently become a part of our educational experience. But the term conveys further meanings implying precision of style [and] formality of structure" (Harry Levin, Introduction to *The Scarlet Letter and Other Tales of the Puritans*).

- "There are many reasons why certain works of literature are classics, and most of them are purely literary reasons. But there's another reason too: a great work of literature is also a place in which the whole cultural history of the nation that produced it comes into focus" (Northrop Frye, *The Educated Imagination*).

- A classic "modifies our very being and makes us feel . . . we are not the same men and women we were when we began it" (Sheldon Sacks, *Fiction and the Shape of Belief*).

- A classic "lays its images permanently on the mind [and] is entirely irreplaceable in the sense that no other book whatever comes anywhere near reminding you of it or being even a momentary substitute for it" (C. S. Lewis, review of *Taliessin through Logres*).

- The classics "deal with the archetypes of human experience, with characters at once concrete and universal, and with events and relationships that are invariant in the lives of all men. . . . The perils of the soul and its achievements are constant. From his earliest literary efforts man does not seem to have advanced in

The classics are so great that they often remain a permanent part of us even if we read them only once in school. A literary critic has written that "the classics are books that exert a peculiar influence, both when they refuse to be eradicated from the mind and when they conceal themselves in the folds of memory" (Italo Calvino, "Why Read the Classics?").

his comprehension of them, and may well have declined" (Kenneth Rexroth, Introduction to *Classics Revisited*).

- "Among the best of a class; of the highest quality in a group. . . . A literary classic, then, ranks with the best of its kind that have been produced" (*The Harper Handbook to Literature*).

- "A piece of literature which by common consent has achieved a recognized position in literary history for its superior qualities; also an author of like standing. Thus *Paradise Lost* is a *classic* in English literature" (Thrall and Hibbard's *Handbook to Literature*).

- A classic "is doubly *permanent*: for it remains significant, or it acquires a new significance, after the age for which it was written and the conditions under which it was written, have passed away; and yet it keeps, undefaced by handling, the original noble imprint of the mind that first minted it" (Arthur Quiller-Couch, "On the Use of Masterpieces," in *On the Art of Reading*).

- "The classics are books that come down to us bearing the traces of readings previous to ours, and bringing in their wake the traces they themselves have left on the culture or cultures they have passed through" (Italo Calvino, "Why Read the Classics?" in *The Uses of Literature*).

Until recently, certain agreed-upon classics formed the core of the literature curriculum at both high school and college levels. This aggregate of works was known as the "canon"—the definitive list of works that any educated person knew. With the collapse of the old culture, the canon has become so eroded that it is hard to come up with a list of masterworks for a series like Crossway's Christian Guides to the Classics (authored by Leland Ryken). Many leading English departments no longer have a list of required courses that all English majors must take, or works that students are expected to know.

The first thing to note about these definitions is how little overlap there is. This should alert us to the fact that we are dealing with a many-faceted phenomenon. We can regard the differences among the definitions as reflecting what each of the authors regards as the primary or most obvious trait of a classic. Probably none of the people who formulated the definitions would disagree with the other definitions.

As the definitions show, the concept of a classic combines an objective, verifiable aspect and a subjective element that is personal to the experience or perception of an individual. One of the objective criteria is *endurance*. A classic has stood the test of time and yet is still current. It is both timeless and timely. Unlike a classic car, which sometimes immediately strikes us as dated when we see it, a literary classic is only superficially dated. It actually lives on. People who sneer at the classics and their authors as being "dead" miss the point: the classics are like Abel, who "though he died . . . still speaks" (Heb. 11:4).

The fact that historical continuity and permanence are required before we call something a classic explains why a literary work does not immediately attain the full status of being a classic. It may possess the quality of excellence that entitles it eventually to be called a classic, but the ESPN Classic sports channel is not quite right in calling the previous day's game "an instant classic." The original book reviews of C. S. Lewis's Chronicles of Narnia were extraordinarily positive, but the Narnia stories did not fully establish themselves as classics until they had been on the scene for a decade or two.

A second objective criterion for a classic is that it is *influential* in the cultures that embrace it, starting with the culture that produced it. As part of this permanent influence, classics have historically been part of the educational program of cultures. This extends not only to what happens in schools but also in families (where education be-

In 1987, E. D. Hirsch Jr. published a bestselling book, *Cultural Literacy: What Every American Needs to Know.* In it he made the case for the benefits to society of educating every child and citizen in a shared body of essential information. Cultural literacy of this type is broader than just the literary classics, but the literary classics are an important part of the cultural literacy that Hirsch and his supporters envision. Hirsch repeatedly stresses that it is the currently disadvantaged that have the most to gain by becoming culturally literate and able to participate in society.

gins). Often the classics have formed the core of the educational curricula of a society. This applies to all of the academic disciplines, so that law and biology and history (for example) all have their classic texts.

We do not personally need to like every literary classic, but even when we do not like a given classic, we acknowledge its importance as a cultural phenomenon. As a literature teacher, I teach and would defend the classic status of some works that I personally do not enjoy and would not choose to read on my own initiative. But in keeping with what I have said about the cultural importance of a classic, when I leave a given classic unread, I am aware of a cultural gap and deficiency at that point. This cultural significance of the classics shows that at some level, they are indispensable to societies and to individuals who claim to be part of their cultures.

The most universally agreed upon component of a literary classic is the criterion of *excellence* or superiority. This extends to both the form and content of the work. A classic rises above most other members of its class. Thus Homer's epics are the best Greek epics, and Shakespeare's tragedies are the best of Renaissance drama. This ingredient of excellence quickly reaches out to encompass other qualities. For example, to rise to the top, literary works need to possess a certain multiplicity and richness. They become central to a culture or curriculum because literary critics can do a lot with them. They have a density of technique and content that make them inexhaustible. By comparison, ordinary works seem a little thin, no matter how much we personally might enjoy them.

There continue to be those who believe that the classics should remain central to a literary curriculum. One of them writes, "The heart of any good curriculum in literature must be what has proved through the ages its wearability, and its power to liberate, illuminate, and support" (Helen Gardner, *In Defence of the Imagination*).

We should note two further things about the criterion of excellence. The fact that classics are the best of a group or category explains why the word has become a standard honorific adjective. When people want to praise something or garner a market for it, they readily resort to calling it a classic. Second, the mere fact that something has been around for a long time does not make it a classic. A kooky-looking car can be a collectible and an antique, but a car needs to be beautiful and shapely to rank as a classic.

An additional subjective test for a classic literary work is that it *touches us at a profound level*. Before we willingly call a work a classic, we need to be deeply affected by it. To meet the test fully, the work needs to be a landmark in our intellectual, spiritual, and literary experience. If it does not rise to that stature, our granting it the title of *classic* is just a little halfhearted.

One of the traits of the classics is that they are inexhaustible—not only for individual readers over the course of their lifetime with its changing experiences, but also in the sense that successive cultures see different things in a classic, based on their own experiences and worldviews. Homer's original audience relished the battle scenes that figure prominently in his stories; today we are likely to be repelled by such violence.

Chapter Summary

The following definition does a good job of incorporating the threads that have been woven in this chapter's definition of a classic literary work. To achieve this distinction, the definition is a long one that keeps expanding:

> "What we tend to require for something called a literary [classic] is a display of great craftsmanship [and] . . . striking originality. . . . Beyond this . . . the text must make a powerful emotional and intellectual impact, provide a rich reading experience, and leave behind a larger understanding of our past experience and perhaps a new way to think about our lives. In the case of the greatest works we return to them time

and again in our minds, even if we do not reread them frequently, as touchstones by which we interpret the world around us." (Nina Baym, *The Scarlet Letter: A Reading*)

CHAPTER 3

Why We Should Read the Classics

There are some things in life whose value is apparent if we simply understand what they are. The classics are one of these. Implicit in the definitions of a classic provided in the preceding chapter are reasons for wanting to read and possess the classics. The purpose of this chapter is to make those reasons explicit.

The Entertainment Value of the Classics

The first reason to read the classics will surprise some people. It is that the classics provide superior entertainment for the people who have developed a taste for them. I myself prefer the classics because I find them more entertaining than other forms of reading.

I need to make some immediate concessions on this point. First, I am by profession a teacher of literature. Naturally, I like to read Dickens and Browning and Chaucer. But I have known many people in my life who are not literature teachers and yet enjoy reading the classics.

I will also concede that the taste for the classics is partly an acquired taste, especially in a day when, if left to their own designs, children

The hedonistic defense of literature (defending literature on the pleasure principle) is as old as literary theory. The most customary word that writers have used to name the pleasure-giving aspect of literature is the word *delight*, and often it has been paired with truth or wisdom to form a twofold defense of literature. The author of Ecclesiastes tells us that he "sought to find words of delight, and uprightly he wrote words of truth" (12:10). Romantic English poet Percy Shelley called poetry "a fountain for ever overflowing with the waters of wisdom and delight" (*A Defense of Poetry*). Shelley's definition is a good summary of what the literary classics give us.

gravitate to video games, young people to movies, and adults to television viewing. The fact that
our culture encourages these behaviors does not
mean that we need to succumb to them. A main
purpose of education in the schools and in the
family, to say nothing of self-education, should be
to instill the taste that allows people to enjoy the
classics. Most people in our culture settle for a low
standard in their leisure-time pursuits. We are a
lazy society—physically, mentally, imaginatively,
and spiritually. Christians do not need to settle
for that.

To defend the classics because they bring
enjoyment is to defend them on hedonistic
grounds—defending them because they give us
pleasure. (I will note in passing that two other
defenses of literature have been important in the
history of thinking about literature and the arts;
they are the utilitarian defense that literature is
useful and the moral defense that literature leads
people to good behavior.) T. S. Eliot once called
great literature "superior amusement" (Introduction to *The Sacred Wood*). The word *entertainment*
is perhaps better: the classics provide superior entertainment.

Again I will make a concession to people who
are not yet fully committed to the classics: for
people who have had the classics foisted on them
before they were ready to enjoy them, reading a
classic can seem more like a duty than a pleasure.
Additionally, when we first start to read a sophisticated, difficult, or long classic, we might do so with
a sense of duty. But these challenges are not an
indictment of the classics themselves. Instead of
moping, we need to get started with a given classic,

We most naturally
think of the superior-
ity of the classics as
consisting of their form
and technique rather
than their subject
matter and content.
But even the content
of a classic is superior.
Why do we hang repro-
ductions of paintings
by the masters on our
walls? We choose them
over original paintings
because, even in
reproduction, we value
their superior design
and subject matter.

knowing that this is a prerequisite to moving from duty to pleasure.

What makes a classic work of literature entertaining? The ingredients that make up a work of literature are the things that potentially make it pleasurable and entertaining. One of the tasks of literature is to present human experience for us—to hold the mirror up to nature, as Shakespeare's fictional character Hamlet states it. Some literary and artistic subject matter is more entertaining than other content. We are talking about striking and interesting events, characters, settings, meditations, and emotions. The classics win us partly by giving us exceptional and attention-grabbing content.

Even more important is the aspect of literary form and technique (about which I will say more in a moment). Some readers are aware of this dimension of the works they read, while others simply read with no awareness of the writer's technique. But both categories share the quality of enjoying the writer's cultivation of the resources of literary art and skill. Interestingly, unsophisticated readers who know little about literary matters tend to gravitate toward literature that possesses superior technique.

The first reason to value the classics and make room for them in our leisure time is that they are fun to read. Milton's epic *Paradise Lost* is a long and formidable epic that may seem the kind of work that we read for edification rather than fun. I therefore commend what the Inkling Charles Williams said about the effect that stems from Milton's writing his masterwork in poetic form rather than prose. Williams wrote, "*Paradise Lost* is much more fun written in blank verse than it would be in prose, or is so to any one capable of enjoying that particular kind of fun. Let us have all the delights of which we are capable" (*Reason and Beauty in the Poetic Mind*).

Superior Technique and Artistry

I have already hinted at a second mark in favor of the classics. It is that they possess a greater degree of artistic excellence than lesser works. The right term for this ingredient in a work of literature is literary form—the "how" of a piece as distinct from the "what" (the content). The specifics of literary form vary from one genre to another, but the principles that underlie all the manifestations include unity, coherence, progression, repetition, balance, symmetry, contrast, and clarity combined with multiplicity. The catch-all aesthetic term that experts through the ages have used to cover this quality is *beauty*. These same experts sometimes speak of writers or artists or composers as exploiting the resources of technique that belong to their specific art form.

It is easy to see why literature teachers prefer works that possess an abundance of literary technique: there is so much that they can do with such works when explicating them in the classroom. But nonteachers also reap the benefits of superior artistry. A student writing a paper has more to say about a work with density and richness of technique than a work that carries all its meaning on the surface and is devoid of artistic skill. Even a reader who knows little about literary form responds to it. Why did the Sherlock Holmes and Miss Marple mysteries rise to the top among readers of murder mysteries? Because they are better written than many others. Their authors were better at description and character creation and had a way with words that make their stories more winsome than mysteries with equally inventive plots.

Why should we read the classics? They offer us more beauty, artistry, and formal excellence than ordinary literature possesses. They have an added aesthetic element.

The Portrayal of Human Experience

It is a truism that the subject of literature is human experience concretely portrayed. Teachers of creative writing tell their students that the task of the literary author is to show rather than tell. To *show* means to render the subject matter as concretely as possible. To *tell* is to state abstractions. When storytellers or poets show us what life is like, they just naturally present human experience in a form that we imaginatively and vicariously relive it. The fuller or richer the portrayal of life is, the more profoundly we feel that we have entered into essential human experience.

Literature as a whole is the human race's testimony to its own experience. Some portrayals of experience strike us as thin and surface level. Others meet a criterion that a Victorian enthusiast for the classics, Matthew Arnold, famously bequeathed when he claimed that the classics touch upon life "with extraordinary power at an unusual number of points" ("Literature and Science"). To "touch upon life" means that readers feel they have been taken inside the very essence of the human experiences that an author has chosen to put before them.

This is one of the points at which the classics show their superiority over lesser literature. The great writers have the ability to capture the essence

> The greatness of a classic consists of both its form and content. Matthew Arnold wrote that in the classics "the substance and matter on the one hand, the style and manner on the other, have a mark, an accent, of high beauty, worth, and power" ("The Study of Poetry").

of human experience. They are the voice of authentic human experience. A bumper-sticker mentality tells the world that "LIFE SUCKS; THEN YOU DIE." But in his novel *The Stranger*, Albert Camus leads us to feel what it is like to live in a universe in which a person finds life meaningless. A television detective drama gets us to relive an exciting sequence of events and leaves us with no insight into the nature of evil and justice, while a Shakespearean tragedy gets to the heart of those issues.

All that I say in this chapter in defense of the classics is on my list of "most important things to say," but perhaps the matter of profundity of insight into human experience tops the list. The profundity of which I speak consists of the presentation of human experience, not in the presentation of ideas (which I do not disparage). This ability to reproduce human experience at its deepest level is something that the classics share with the Bible.

Demanding the Best from Us

I have already ascribed qualities to classics that prepare the way for me to assert my next point. It is that the classics, not counting popular forms such as nursery rhymes and folktales, possess a quality of complexity, density, and multiplicity of levels. This being the case, the classics demand more from us as readers than lesser works do. By demanding more from us, the classics can be said to elicit our best effort. This is a mark in their favor.

In turn, if the classics elicit more from us, they offer us greater rewards than works that carry all of their meaning on the surface and require little effort from us. This is simply a principle of life. In my experience as a college literature teacher, I have repeatedly found that my students do their

> The classics are part of the human quest for the greatest and best. Matthew Arnold claimed that in our literary experience "we must accustom ourselves to a high standard. . . . The best poetry is what we want; the best poetry will be found to have a power of forming, sustaining, and delighting us, as nothing else can." Arnold also said that if a poet "is a real classic, if his work belongs to the class of the very best (for this is the true and right meaning of the word *classic* . . .), then the great thing for us is to feel and enjoy his work as deeply as ever we can" ("The Study of Poetry").

best work with difficult writers like Shakespeare and Milton. I absolutely love students who elicit my best effort in the classroom. The classics can serve a similar role in our reading experience: they demand the most from us and, in the process, enrich us the most.

Encountering the Great Ideas

I somewhat dread to embark on the subject of the ideas that the classics embody because so many enthusiasts of the classics have reduced them to their ideas. To do so is to distort the nature of literature. If the ideas of literature were the really important thing, we would not need to read literature at all; we could simply compile a list of ideas and proceed to discuss them. C. S. Lewis has written well on this subject. To regard a work of literature "as primarily a vehicle for . . . philosophy," writes Lewis in his book *An Experiment in Criticism*, "is an outrage to the thing the poet has made for us. . . . One of the prime achievements in every good fiction has nothing to do with truth or philosophy . . . at all."

This does not mean, however, that we should neglect the ideas that the classics put on our intellectual agenda. In fact, this is one of their greatest services to us. The classics, especially the masterworks of substantial length, are as good an avenue to encountering the great issues of life as we will find. The masters who produced the classics were great thinkers and should be honored as such. Furthermore, they had a knack for posing life's questions in a form that makes their ideas easy to discern, explore, and debate.

There is a perennial fallacy that we need to note as we celebrate the ability of the classics to embody the worldviews by which people have lived. It has been easy for people to make a facile equation of ideas with truth. Because the masterworks embody ideas, this line of thought says, they tell us the truth. But obviously, ideas can be false as well as true. The usefulness of encountering ideas in the classics is not necessarily that these works tell us the truth, but rather that, by posing the great issues of life, the classics serve as a catalyst to our thinking about those ideas. Whether by agreement or disagreement with the ideas that we encounter in the classics, we sharpen our own understanding of the truth and are affirmed in it. It is not necessarily a matter of literature telling us the truth, but rather of our *coming to understand and affirm the truth* as we read the classics and interact with their ideas.

The Classics as Our Contact with the Past

A final value of reading the classics is the one that requires the most analysis. Most of the classics we read come to us from the past, and often the distant past. Therein lies one of their chief uses to us, but we need to define the issues clearly.

I begin with a caution: it is not the pastness of the classics that makes these works classics, nor is there anything automatically meritorious about the past. Many other works that come from the past do not rise to the status of being classics. In fact, the mere fact that a classic is remote from us in time does not by itself contribute anything at all to making the work a classic. Additionally, many classics are only a few years old and belong to the modern and even contemporary milieu.

Having asserted that the classics are our gateway to the past, the next question becomes why we

"Why are we reading, if not in hope of beauty laid bare, life heightened and its deepest mystery probed? Can the writer isolate and vivify all in experience that most deeply engages our intellects and our hearts? Can the writer renew our hope for literary forms? Why are we reading if not in hope that the writer will . . . illuminate and inspire us with wisdom, courage, and the possibility of meaningfulness, and will press upon our minds the deepest mysteries, so we may feel again their majesty and power?" (Annie Dillard, *The Writing Life*).

should cultivate a knowledge of the past. There are multiple reasons. The first is related to the fact that the classics are characterized as being *the best*. It is verifiable that many of the greatest and best things belong to the past. The great cathedrals were built centuries ago. So were castles and palaces. Many of the greatest paintings, sculptures, and pieces of music are centuries old.

The same is true of literature. The Victorian apologist for the classics, Matthew Arnold, correctly said that thinking people want contact with "the best that is known and thought in the world" ("The Function of Criticism at the Present Time"). That being true, we will naturally turn to the literary classics of the past because, in sheer numbers, most of the greatest works have predated our own age. To evoke the honorable triad called *the true, the good, and the beautiful*, we can say that we are more likely to encounter these three things in the classics of the past than in modern and contemporary works of literature. There are many exceptions in the dual sense that some works from the past do not give us the true, the good, and the beautiful, while some modern ones do. This does not negate the principle that we value our excursions into the classics of the past because they represent the best that has been thought and expressed.

In addition, we read the classics from the past because they liberate us from bondage to the contemporary. Several great scholars have written very well on this subject, but none better than C. S. Lewis. His most famous discourse on this topic was a sermon that he preached during the Second World War titled "Learning in War-Time." Having asserted that "we need intimate knowledge of the past," Lewis immediately adds, "Not that the past

One result of taking excursions into the literature of the past is that we put ourselves in touch with what is permanent in human experience. T. S. Eliot claimed that "the historical sense involves a perception, not only of the pastness of the past, but of its presence" ("Tradition and the Individual Talent"). Wendell Berry wrote that "if we fail to see that we live in the same world that Homer lived in, then we not only misunderstand Homer; we misunderstand ourselves." By seeing what is constant, Berry believes, we understand "the necessities and values that are the foundation of our life" (*Standing by Words*).

has any magic about it, but because we ... need something to set against the present." Then he famously gives the following analogy: "A man who has lived in many places is not likely to be deceived by the local errors of his native village: the [person who knows the past] has lived in many times and is therefore in some degree immune from the great cataract of nonsense that pours from the press and the microphone of his own age." (See also Lewis's essay "On the Reading of Old Books" in *God in the Dock*; also easily found online.)

Knowledge of the past can serve as a ballast against the contemporary. Literary critic Northrop Frye claimed that when we read literature from the past, "we are led into a different kind of culture, with unfamiliar assumptions, beliefs, and values." Further, contact with this unfamiliar world "is what expands our own view of human possibilities" (*Spiritus Mundi: Essays on Literature, Myth, and Society*). G. K. Chesterton famously said that "tradition means giving votes to the most obscure of all classes, our ancestors. It is the democracy of the dead. . . . Democracy tells us not to neglect a good man's opinion," no matter who he is (*Orthodoxy*).

And there is yet a further twist: when we see how differently the human race thought and acted in the past, we simultaneously see how differently we think and act compared to our forebears. T. S. Eliot wrote that a historical sense is what makes a person "most acutely conscious of his place in time, of his own contemporaneity" ("Tradition and the Individual Talent"). Sometimes we conclude that on a given matter people from the past exceeded us, while in other instances we prefer our own ways of thinking and doing, but in both cases it is our encounter with the past that serves as the catalyst to clarify our thinking.

There is even one more twist: when we take a journey into the classics of the past, we are surprised to see how contemporary they are. This is true because the classics have a particular knack for capturing what is universal in human experience. The principle underlying this continuity and permanence is tradition. Because a tradition is permanent, it can serve as a standard by which to measure aberrations, especially those that are pushed upon us by a secular culture that has lost its way.

Along these lines, contemporary author Wendell Berry has said that "our past is not merely something to depart from; it is to commune with, to speak with" (*Standing by Words*). "The past is our definition," writes Berry—a permanent standard of what it means to be human and live the good life. Without such "a live tradition, we are necessarily the prey of fashion." Literary critic Helen Gardner uses the same terminology in defending the classics: "Studying the literature of past ages . . . demands that for a while we lay aside our own concerns, prejudices, and opinions and enter into the experiences of other [times]." As a result, "the study of the literature of past ages . . . enables us . . . to discover for ourselves standards of permanence which can save us from the domination of [contemporary] fashion" ("The Relevance of Literature," in *In Defence of the Imagination*).

The farther contemporary culture departs from the traditional moorings of the past, the more subversive the classics become. The classics do not confirm accepted prejudices but challenge them. The attack on the classics by "politically correct"

The whole drift of this chapter on the value of reading the classics is to entice people to enter the world of literary classics. What happens to people who refuse that invitation? C. S. Lewis, in his book *An Experiment in Criticism*, pictures such people as living an impoverished life of missed opportunities. He writes, "Those of us who have been true readers all our life seldom fully realise the enormous extension of our being which we owe to authors. We realise it best when we talk with an unliterary friend. . . . The man who is contented to be only himself . . . is in prison."

liberals has gotten the situation exactly wrong. It is their propaganda mill that mechanically reinforces the stock responses of contemporary young people. By contrast, virtually everything that the classics assert becomes more revolutionary with every passing year.

Chapter Summary

The values that the classics offer us flow from the nature of the classics themselves. As I summarize the five main points of this chapter, I will suggest how a Christian mind-set can assess each value.

- The Christian faith affirms the enjoyment and pleasure that the classics offer us.
- God is the ultimate author of the artistry and beauty that are a hallmark of the classics.
- The example of the Bible shows that God values human experience and, by implication, approves the way in which the classics deepen our understanding of it.
- God is the God of truth, so of course he delights when we are led to embrace truth as we interact with the ideas embodied in the classics.
- Because the great events on which the Christian faith rests happened long ago, and because the sacred book of the Christian faith is thousands of years old, drawing strength from the past as we do when we read the classics is an orientation that is natural for Christians.

CHAPTER 4
The Greatest Classic: The Bible

This chapter serves several purposes in the design of this book, *A Christian Guide to the Classics*. Since it is a short book like the other books in this series, I do not have the leisure to explore in detail how various aspects of my discussion relate to the Christian faith. This chapter enables me to say in kernel form the most important things that need to be said by way of such integration.

Additionally, readers who have been resistant to what I have said in favor of the classics up to this point will, I think, be inclined to accept my praise of the classics when they consider that the Bible meets all the criteria of what constitutes a classic. Finally, I myself am led to see certain things about other classics when I analyze the ways in which the Bible is a classic, and about the Bible when I apply to it what I know about other classics generally.

The Greatest Classic

One trait that characterizes every true classic is that successive cultures recognize and acknowledge its importance for a society and the individuals in it. The first published statement among English-speaking people that declared the English Bible to be a classic can be found in *McGuffey's Fifth Eclectic Reader*, which called the Bible "the best of classics the world has ever admired." That was certainly not the last of such statements, but before I note some additional ones, I need to clarify that these statements have the King James Version in view.

Those of my readers who are accustomed to

We need to acknowledge a certain complexity with calling the Bible *the supreme literary classic.* The centrality of the Bible in Western culture exists quite apart from a specific English translation. However, when we move to the literary qualities of the Bible, apart from its cultural influence, we need to be aware that we are talking about the King James Version and modern translations in that tradition, not translations that sell that birthright of excellence for something unliterary.

using a dynamic equivalent or colloquial Bible might well be perplexed by the quotations that I will shortly share. Only some English translations result in a Bible that merits the praise that the experts shower on the King James Bible. We can rightly speak of the King James *tradition* that includes three twentieth-century translations—the Revised Standard Version, the New King James Version, and the English Standard Version. Other modern translations, while useful in their particular spheres, do not retain the stylistic excellence of the King James tradition. Instead, they make the Bible read like the daily newspaper and the chatter at the corner coffeeshop. No classic sounds like those things. To make this personal, I could not have my career as a specialist in the Bible as literature if my only translation options had been dynamic equivalent and colloquial translations.

Here, then, are further tributes to the status of the English Bible as a classic in English-speaking cultures:

- Book titles include *The Supreme Book of Mankind*, *The Greatest English Classic*, and *The Book of Books*.
- "No other book has so penetrated and permeated the hearts and speech of the English race" (Adam Nicolson, *God's Secretaries*).
- "The Authorized Version is a miracle and a landmark. . . . There is no corner of English life, no conversation ribald or reverent that it has not adorned" (J. Isaacs, an essay in *The Bible in Its Ancient and English Versions*).
- "If everything else in our language should perish it would alone suffice to show the whole extent of its beauty and power"

An expert on Bible translations says, regarding the KJV, that "it grew to be a national possession and . . . is, in truth, a national classic" (Albert S. Cook, *The Cambridge History of English Literature*). Someone else writes that "in popular Christian culture, the King James translation is seen to possess a dignity and authority" that are unique among English Bible translations (Alister McGrath, *In the Beginning*).

(Thomas Babington Macaulay, *Miscellaneous Writings*).

- "The King James Bible retains its place as a literary and religious classic, by which all others continue to be judged" (Alister McGrath, *In the Beginning*).

What these tributes show is the supreme status of the Bible as a classic. It is not simply *a* classic but *the* classic. While the quoted statements come from literary experts, the Bible has been the possession of common people to an extent unmatched by any other classic. It has been more widely read than any other book in the world. It is the world's all-time best seller, and some sources claim that it is still the best-selling book in the world.

The Bible as Literature

But is the Bible a *literary* classic (the subject of this book)? Yes, it is. It meets all the criteria that make a text literary. For at least a century it has been common to designate this aspect of the Bible with the formula "the Bible as literature."

Before I confirm the accuracy of that label, I want to dispel four misconceptions that might be obstacles to accepting the literary nature of the Bible. (1) To view the Bible as literature is not a modern idea, nor does it need to imply theological liberalism. The idea of the Bible as literature began with the writers of the Bible, who display literary qualities in their writings and who refer with technical precision to a wide range of literary genres such as psalm, proverb, parable, and apocalypse. (2) Although fictionality is a common trait of literature, it is not an essential feature of it. A work of literature can be replete with literary technique

According to popular history, American pioneers sometimes had two books in their covered wagons as they traveled westward—the King James Bible and the complete works of Shakespeare. If true, this tells us something important: the pioneers were aware that they were preserving the literary, cultural, and linguistic tradition that they regarded as a foundation of their civilization.

and artifice while remaining historically factual. (3) To approach the Bible as literature need not entail viewing it *only* as literature, any more than reading it as history requires us to see only the history of the Bible. (4) When we see literary qualities in the Bible we are not attempting to bring the Bible down to the level of ordinary literature; it is simply an objective statement about the inherent nature of the Bible. The Bible can be trusted to reveal its extraordinary qualities if we approach it with ordinary methods of literary analysis.

With potential objections thus laid to rest, we can proceed to identify the literary traits of the Bible, starting at the level of content or subject matter. The impulse of literary authors is to present human experience as concretely as possible, not to present ideas in philosophic or theological form. Literature enacts rather than summarizes. It is a picture of life, not a collection of ideas about life. Literature is an incarnation of human experience, and as such it "shows" rather than "tells" (the common formula used by teachers of literature and imaginative writing as they distinguish the method of concretion from the method of abstract generalizing).

While the Bible is not wholly literary in its content, it is overwhelmingly so. Its stories show us characters in action in specific settings. Its poems speak a language of images. Its visions are filled with concrete pictures that we see in our imaginations. The Bible is not a theological outline with proof texts attached. The sixth commandment states propositionally, "You shall not murder." The story of Cain and Abel incarnates that truth in character and action, without even using the ab-

"The Bible is a book-making book. It is literature which provokes literature. . . . The first and most notable fact regarding the influence of the Bible on English literature is the remarkable extent of that influence. It is literally everywhere" (C. Boyd McAfee, *The Greatest English Classic*).

straction *murder*. At least 80 percent of the Bible is literary in this way.

A second way in which the Bible meets literary criteria is the preponderance of literary genres that we find within its covers. The overall format of the Bible is that of the literary anthology—a collection of individual works composed by multiple authors and falling into familiar literary categories. The dominant genre is narrative or story. Poetry is the next most prevalent genre. Both of those fall into dozens of subtypes—hero story, tragedy, parable, praise psalm, love poem, and so forth. In the Bible we find satire, visionary writing, epistles, and proverbs. Despite its unique features, the anthology that we know as the Bible (a word that means "little books") is thoroughly familiar to people who have had experience with literary anthologies like *The Norton Anthology of English Literature*.

In addition to taking human experience as its subject matter and packaging it in familiar literary genres, the Bible is literary in its style. Regardless of its specific genre, a literary text displays special resources of language that set it apart from ordinary expository writing. Literary writing flaunts its figures of speech, its rhetorical patterning (with techniques such as repetition and contrast), and its stylistic flair. Literary authors are wordsmiths, and their writing has an aphoristic sparkle that makes it striking and unforgettable. The Bible is the most aphoristic book that we know, and it naturally rises to the level of literary discourse as a result.

More could be said about the literary nature of the Bible, but all that is required here is to establish the place of the Bible in the category

Many literary scholars have commented on the biblical writers' practice of avoiding the abstract in preference to the concrete. Here is a specimen statement: "In Hebrew . . . the vocabulary was consciously pictorial and concrete in its character. . . . The Biblical vocabulary is compact of the primal stuff of our common humanity— of its universal emotional, sensory experiences" (John Livingston Lowes, "The Noblest Monument of English Prose").

that this book covers, namely literary classics. A good summary statement comes from C. S. Lewis: "There is a . . . sense in which the Bible, since it is after all literature, cannot properly be read except as literature; and the different parts of it as the different sorts of literature they are" (*Reflections on the Psalms*).

The Centrality of the Bible as a Cultural Presence

We know a classic partly by the commanding role that it plays in a culture. A classical scholar has said regarding Homer that "the important question is not who Homer was, but *what* he was. The *Iliad* and the *Odyssey* have been called the Bible of the Greeks. For centuries these two poems were the basis of Greek education. . . . A citation from Homer was the natural way of settling a question of morals or behavior. . . . Homer held and nourished the minds and imaginations of Greeks for generation after generation—of artists, thinkers, and ordinary simple men alike" (H. D. F. Kitto, *The Greeks*). A Christian who reads that description almost automatically makes a connection to the Bible.

In *Postmodern Theology*, retired Yale University professor George Lindbeck paints a helpful picture of the way in which the Bible has functioned as the most important classic in English-speaking cultures through the centuries. Until recently, writes Lindbeck, "most people in traditionally Christian cultures lived in the linguistic and imaginative world of the Bible." Even uneducated and non-Christian people "knew the actual text from Genesis to Revelation." The Bible was an omnipresent cultural frame of reference. It provided "the conceptual and imaginative vocabu-

Some of the greatest tributes to the Bible come from English literary authors. One of them is the Romantic poet Samuel Taylor Coleridge: "In the Bible there is more that *finds* me than I have experienced in all other books put together. . . . The words of the Bible find me at greater depths of my being" (*Confessions of an Enquiring Spirit*). Elsewhere Coleridge asked, "Did you ever meet any book that went to your heart so often and so deeply?" (*Notebooks*).

laries ... with which [people construed] reality." Lindbeck concludes that the Bible was so pervasive "that much of western literature consists of subtexts of the biblical text." Lindbeck's summary statement is that "Christendom dwelt imaginatively in the biblical world."

One of Lindbeck's points is the literary influence of the Bible, and this needs to be highlighted. An essential feature of a classic is that it lives on in subsequent literature, art, and music. The Bible has done just that. Literary scholar Northrop Frye has called the Bible "the major informing influence on literary symbolism" (*Anatomy of Criticism*). T. R. Henn, in his book *The Bible as Literature*, writes that the Bible "becomes one with the Western tradition, because it is its greatest source." (For a full treatment of the Bible as a literary masterpiece and its influence on English and American literature, see Leland Ryken, *The Legacy of the King James Bible*.)

The Bible "flavored the common man's speech, inspired the artist's brush, determined the poet's imagery, bestowed purpose upon a people. It is *the* book" (Edwin S. Gaustad, *The Religious History of America*).

The Bible and the Classics

The foregoing discussion is scarcely more than a summary of important principles. It will suffice, though, as a foundation for the following analysis of how the Bible functions in relation to the literary classics in general.

First, the Bible is the central authority for Christians. Christianity is a revealed religion, meaning that it derives its beliefs from a book that is regarded as a divine revelation. In the remaining chapters of this book I will discuss how I think Christians should read the classics. One of the points I will make is that Christians need to weigh the truth claims of literary classics by a standard of biblical truth. This is a central function of the Bible in the study of the classics.

Additionally, our reading of the classics generally, along with commentary about them such as I have conducted in the early chapters of this book, can give depth of field to our understanding of the Bible as a literary classic. We start to see additional dimensions to the Bible when we consider the claims that literary scholars make regarding what makes a book a classic. An element of recognition enters our awareness in regard to the Bible.

But there is actually a two-way street between the Bible and other classics. Our own longtime experience with the Bible becomes a frame of reference as we assimilate the things that literary scholars say about the classics. For example, when we consider the impact of the Bible in our lives, we have a deeper appreciation for a statement by a literary scholar that a classic "modifies our very being," or that a classic "is entirely irreplaceable" for us.

Finally, remaining indifferent to the value of literary classics is not a genuine option if we consider that the Bible is a literary classic. The status of the Bible as a literary classic validates the idea of the classics, just as the fact that it is literary validates literature itself.

> "The simplicity of the Bible is the simplicity of majesty, not of equality, much less of naiveté: its simplicity expresses the voice of authority" (Northrop Frye, *The Great Code*).

Chapter Summary

The Bible is the greatest and most influential classic in the English-speaking world. It is a thoroughly literary book and therefore ranks as a literary classic. It has exerted the cultural influence that characterizes the greatest classics. It is the standard of truth by which Christians measure the truth claims of other classics.

CHAPTER 5

How Not to Read a Classic

The foregoing chapters have defined what a classic is and have given reasons for valuing the classics. The logical next step is to move from the nature of the classics to a methodology for reading them. Upon reflection, we can see that it is as important to be on guard against bad practices in regard to the classics as it is to read them in the right ways. This chapter takes a look at bad practices and attitudes that can derail us in our journey through the classics.

Bad Practice #1: *Treat the reading of a classic as a solemn duty—something that you are required to do instead of desire to do.*

Before we criticize the "duty" way of reading a classic, we should pause to analyze why it is easy to fall into this attitude. We are aware from the start that a classic is something great—something that belongs to a very elite circle. Furthermore, most people are introduced to the classics in school, where the reading of them is a course requirement and therefore a duty. And lastly, even though upon reflection we can see that a classic does not need to be a long masterwork like a novel or epic or play, we nonetheless tend to equate a classic with a long and difficult work, and therefore something that we would undertake from utilitarian motives rather than as a leisure-time pleasure. We need to find ways to counteract the "duty theory" of reading the classics; if we don't, we will leave them behind the day we graduate from school.

We can begin by recalling that the Bible is the

C. S. Lewis's book *An Experiment in Criticism* (his only book of literary theory) is a gold mine of good thinking on many aspects of literature. One of them is the entertainment value of literature. Lewis wrote, "Every good book should be entertaining. A good book will be more; it must not be less."

greatest classic. Is it a difficult book? Yes. Do we read it because we feel a duty to read it? Yes. But if that is all, we feel that there is "something wrong with this picture." We can develop an attitude of finding Bible reading a pleasure that we want to pursue. The same is true of the classics.

The attitude of obligation arises partly from the fact that we know that the classics are a repository of great ideas. Many classroom teachers stress this aspect, with the result that we view reading the classics as being akin to attending a lecture or listening to a sermon. It is not wrong to pay attention to the ideas embodied in the classics, but to foreground that dimension distorts their nature. Authors of the classics have only rarely viewed themselves as primarily teaching their audiences; instead, they view themselves as entertaining their audiences and giving them a pleasant leisure activity.

I remember the shock I felt when I overheard a colleague tell a student that Homer's primary purpose was to instill ideas—"we know that." Well, we don't know that. In his epic *The Odyssey*, Homer includes descriptions of how epics were performed and received in the societies that produced them. We learn that epics were after-dinner entertainment performed in a banquet hall on a festive occasion. They were not lectures in a lecture hall. Here is one of the descriptions: "'What a pleasure it is, my lord,' Odysseus said, 'to hear a singer [epic storyteller] like this, with a divine voice! I declare it is just the perfection of gracious life: good cheer and good temper everywhere, rows of guests enjoying themselves heartily and listening to the music [playing of the harp while the bard chanted the epic], plenty to eat on the table, wine ready in

In *Christian Reflections*, C. S. Lewis wrote that "much bad [literary] criticism . . . results from the efforts of critics to get a work-time result out of something that never aimed at producing more than pleasure." In a similar vein, the Roman author Horace, wrote twenty years before the birth of Christ, "That is how it is with poetry: created and developed to give joy to human hearts" (*The Art of Poetry*). And Victorian apologist for the classics Matthew Arnold quaintly said that the purpose of poetry is "to inspirit and rejoice the reader" (Preface to *Poems*).

the great bowl, and the butler ready to fill your cup whenever you want it. I think that is the best thing men can have.'"

It is up to us as readers to determine why and how we read the classics. The wrong way is to brace ourselves to fulfill a required and perhaps unpleasant social obligation. The right way is to regard ourselves as ready to enjoy a leisure time pursuit. Reading a classic is more like attending a ball game or picnic than listening to a lecture or mowing the lawn.

Bad Practice #2: *Read the classics primarily for their ideas.*

This bad practice goes hand-in-hand with the didactic ("teaching") view of the classics discussed before. After all, only people with a philosophic bent get their kicks out of analyzing ideas. But prompting us to view the classics as a duty is only one of the bad effects that come from focusing on their ideas.

To look upon a work of literature primarily as a repository of ideas distorts the nature of literature. A work of literature has two elements—form and content. The form consists of anything having to do with the "how" of the work—the genre and the ingredients that comprise the genre, the style, the aspects that we readily identify with beauty and entertainment. And even the content cannot be adequately considered to be only ideas. The writer's first task is to present human experience as concretely as possible—to observe life and record it. For most readers, this is far more engaging and enlightening than the interpretive angle (the ideas) that writers impose on the recorded experiences.

None of this is intended to discredit the ideas

Fiction writer Flannery O'Connor wrote a very helpful book of Christian literary theory titled *Mystery and Manners.* On the subject of not allowing ideas to supersede our enjoyment of literature, she wrote, "Last fall I received a letter from a student who said she would be 'graciously appreciative' if I would tell her 'just what enlightenment' I expected her to get from each of my stories. . . . I wrote her back to forget about enlightenment and just try to enjoy them."

that the masterworks embody. It is rather to encourage a sense of balance and proportion in regard to what we should expect from the classics. Not many people will become lifelong readers of the classics if they exaggerate the role of ideas to the neglect of form and the embodiment of human experience.

Bad Practice #3: *Assume that the classics are totally different from other literature*.

I have already suggested that we tend to place the classics in such an elite category that we think of them as unique—totally unlike the literature to which we gravitate as an enjoyable leisure pursuit. Experience shows that it is very easy to seal off the classics in a world separate from literature in general.

We need to resist this inclination, and it is easy to do so. The great storytellers who have given us the classic stories do not bypass what the popular imagination demands. By *popular imagination* I mean the literary preferences that people universally display—the person of sophisticated literary taste and also Joe the mechanic or Julie the hairdresser. The whole cross section of the population likes the same things in a story, such as plot conflict, striking events, memorable characters, suspense, violence, danger, a touch of fantasy or the supernatural, vivid settings, and suchlike. Storytellers such as Shakespeare and Hawthorne give us all of these.

The thing that distinguishes the classics is not that they ignore universal or popular literary taste. What sets them apart is that the writers give us more than the basic template. In Shakespeare's *Macbeth* we find all the stock ingredients of a mur-

One of the landmarks of literary criticism dealing with the integration of literature and the Christian faith is an essay "Religion and Literature" by T. S. Eliot. One of his points is that Christian readers need to avoid being intimidated from disagreeing with the viewpoint of a great writer. At one point Eliot writes that it is a mark of maturity in a Christian reader to be able to say of a great writer, "This is the view of life of a person who was a good observer within his limits . . . but he looked at [life] in a different way from me [as a Christian reader]."

der story, but we also get a profound exploration of sin and guilt. Homer's *Odyssey* gives us an abundance of heart-stopping suspense and danger, but at the end of the story we realize that these stock plot ingredients have shown us essential qualities of the human journey that every person undertakes in life.

Bad Practice #4: *View the classics as being sacred and beyond criticism.*

We live at a time when literature is decreasingly valued and in which most Americans claim not to read a single book during the course of a year. It may therefore seem superfluous to sound a caution about overvaluing the classics, but there are good reasons for the caution. Among the literati who treasure literature and the arts, the possibility always exists that they will give literature and the arts a higher position than they deserve.

There are always people who elevate the arts to the position of a substitute religion. If for a moment we think not of the classics but of popular music and movies, the case can be made that for many people today, these have replaced the pulpit as the main influence on their thinking and values. In Victorian England (the second half of the nineteenth century), as Christianity began to lose its cultural dominance as a belief system, some cultured people made exaggerated claims for the arts. Matthew Arnold's statement of literature as a substitute religion is particularly famous: "More and more mankind will discover that we have to turn to poetry to interpret life for us . . . and most of what now passes for religion and philosophy will be replaced by poetry" ("The Study of Poetry"). It has not happened on a large scale, but sooner or later most of us encounter non-Christians for whom this is true. Additionally, because artistic experience has certain qualities in common with religious experience, it is not uncommon for people to blur the boundaries between the two, in effect making artistic experiences a substitute religion.

Christians too can overvalue the classics. It is entirely possible to regard the classics as being beyond criticism. This most often happens when readers overcredit a non-Christian writer or work that they particularly like. The tendency among some is to claim favorite works and authors for the Christian faith for no better reason than that a person likes them and wants to validate that estimate.

The best way to avoid the practice is to realize that a work can appeal to us on multiple levels. We can endorse a work at the levels of literary form and accuracy in the portrayal of life, without extending that endorsement to the ideas and worldview embodied in a work. To affirm part of a work need not lead us to defend all of it, and to reject part of a work does not require us to reject all of it. We simply need to keep the record clear about pluses and minuses, both to ourselves and to the outside world.

One of the chapters in Tony Reinke's superb book *Lit! A Christian Guide to Reading Books* bears the subtitle "Seven Benefits of Reading Non-Christian Books." The reasons are impeccable and make good additional reading to the arguments contained in this guide.

Bad Practice #5: *Read only Christian classics.*
The Christian classics naturally hold a very special place in the hearts of Christians—such a special place that it is understandable why some Christians want to limit their sojourns through the realms of gold to Christian classics. The counterpart of this devotion to Christian literature is to be suspicious of non-Christian literature and avoid

reading it. But to read only Christian classics results in an unnecessarily confined literary life.

First, God's common grace (of which more will be said in the second half of this book) enables non-Christian writers to express the true, the good, and the beautiful also. Much of the world's greatest literature has been produced by non-Christians, and by virtue of being great, these works have much that can enrich a Christian reader's life. To be cut off from this tradition is to be unjustifiably impoverished.

Second, the writer's task is threefold. One task is to create literary form, technique, artistry, and beauty for a reader's enjoyment. This dimension of literature is neutral in terms of intellectual allegiance, so an erroneous worldview does not enter the picture in regard to it. There is no good reason to impoverish ourselves by closing the door on what such classics stand ready to impart. The second task of the writer is to present human experience for our contemplation. One of the gifts of literary authors (and painters as well) is the ability to observe life and record it accurately. Truthfulness to reality and human experience is one of the qualities of the arts. Here too the author's religious or intellectual orientation is largely inoperative, just as a photographer's worldview does not strongly enter his or her pictures of life.

The point at which a writer's worldview enters the enterprise is the interpretation that a writer imposes on the presented material. As a result of this third task, interpretation, we can deduce ideas and ultimately a worldview from works of literature. Even when the interpretive angle is wrong, we can benefit from encountering the ideas of works authored by non-Christians. We

A university professor of literature has cautioned Christians not to make exaggerated claims for the Christian nature of works that are not actually Christian. He writes that "we must be careful that we distort neither Christianity nor the specific literary works." He warns against attempts "to appropriate forcibly for religious purposes all the currently fashionable literature," adding a snide comment about hauling non-Christian authors "kicking and screaming to the baptismal font" (Joseph H. Summers, "Christian Literary Scholars").

expand our knowledge of the world and culture within which we live. We come to understand the non-Christian mind and life. We sharpen our own understanding and worldview as we interact with alien viewpoints of literature generally and hold the line against them.

Bad Practice #6: *Resolve to see only what the author and original audience saw in a classic.*

Again we can see how this fallacy gets entrenched. Most of the classics come to us from the past. We value them partly because of the knowledge that they impart about the past. In fact, this is one of the great contributions of the classics to our lives. The fallacy consists of seeing *only* what the author and original audience saw. This fallacy even has a technical name—the *intentional fallacy* (the fallacy of limiting what we see in a work to what we infer to be the author's intention).

The process of good reading begins by journeying from our time and place to the world of the work. An important part of entering that world consists of ascertaining the author's intention as well as reconstructing how the original audience likely assimilated the work. We might look upon this as an act of historical imagination, and it is both instructive and delightful to engage our historical imagination.

But literature is not only particularized; it is also universal. Its value is partly that it admits us to the past, but an even greater value is its ability to express what is true for all people in all places at all times. Furthermore, as the classics pass from one generation to the next, readers see new and different things in them. The original audience

---

We cannot talk about the universality of literature without talking about archetypes. Archetypes are the recurrent plot motifs (such as journey and quest), character types (such as hero and trickster), and images (such as light and water) that we find in both literature and life. Archetypes are universal in human experience and therefore in literature. Writers cannot avoid them if they try (but of course they do not try). Carl Jung wrote that archetypes "make up the groundwork of the human psyche. It is only possible to live the fullest life when we are in harmony with these symbols; wisdom is a return to them" (*Psychological Reflections*).

may have missed or misread something in a work. Values change as history unfolds, and we are free to adopt those changes. A classic is like an organism: once it has been created, it takes on a life of its own. Having allowed an author to state his or her viewpoint, we have a right and even an obligation to assert *our* viewpoint.

Chapter Summary

The classics are a treasure, but their effects are not automatic. We need to handle them correctly in order to avoid distorting them or misusing them. In this chapter I have attempted to dissuade readers from doing the following:

- reading the classics as a duty rather than a pleasure;
- reducing classics to ideas;
- separating the classics from our experience of literature generally;
- venerating the classics beyond what they deserve;
- reading only Christian classics; and
- limiting a classic's meaning to its point of origin.

The positive counterpart of these practices will occupy the next chapter.

CHAPTER 6

How to Read a Classic

The rules for reading the classics are basically the same as the rules for reading literature generally.

This is such a large subject that it could sustain a book all by itself. In this chapter I have distilled what I regard as the most important rules. My remarks are slanted toward substantial masterworks such as epics, plays, and novels, but with just a little adjustment, most of what I say applies equally to a poem or short story.

Good Practice #1: *Read a classic with respect for the momentousness of what you are doing.*

Throughout this book I stress the elite class to which a literary work belongs if it is a classic. The classics are the best of the best. In other areas of life, we put ourselves on our best behavior when we attend a special event or meet a distinguished person. The classics represent literature on its best behavior, and as readers of them we should aspire to meet the same standard.

"Books are not absolutely dead things, but do contain a potency of life in them to be as active as that soul was whose progeny they are. . . . A good book is the precious life-blood of a master spirit, embalmed and treasured up." (John Milton, *Areopagitica*).

When we know that a piece of literature is a classic, we should begin with a vote of confidence for the work. This does not mean that we should be indiscriminate in our assessment of it. It means rather that we begin with an awareness that the world at large has regarded the work as a great work. Greatness deserves to be respected and honored. The liberal establishment today attempts to instill an automatic bias against the classics. We need to reject that attempted coercion. Every work of literature is on trial, but at the end of the day we can virtually depend on it that a classic will give us more truth, wisdom, and beauty than lesser literature (and certainly more than the propagandistic literature of the "politically correct" movement).

Good Practice #2: *Understand the nature of the reading situation.*

Four ingredients converge in any reading situation. These are the work itself (the written or acted text), the author, the reader or audience, and the world (including the author's cultural milieu). In his famous book *The Mirror and the Lamp*, literary critic M. H. Abrams bequeathed a diagram that puts these elements in relation to each other (Diagram 6.1).

Diagram 6.1

English Romantic poet Percy Shelley's angle on the experiential and universal dimension of literature was that literature "is the very image of life expressed in its eternal truth" (*A Defense of Poetry*).

It is simply useful to be aware of the multiplicity of the reading situation and the elements and relationships that form it. Reading literature begins with a focus on the work itself (although that has been ignored in recent approaches to literature in the academy). The work itself is only a potential experience, though, and comes to life only as a reader assimilates the work in terms of his or her beliefs and life experiences. An author created the work in the first place and is a presiding presence in the work, and therefore not to be neglected. Because the subject of literature is human experience (with the author's cultural context as part of the picture), we can also relate literature to life. In fact, personal and universal human experience is the most universal context into which we can place a work of literature.

Good reading respects the way in which these elements interact. It strives to maintain a balance among them. Each of the three elements beyond the work itself can be viewed as providing a context within which we can place a work. I will note one more time (partly because current approaches to literature ignore it) that life itself is a context within which we should assimilate a work of literature. People who never develop the knack of seeing recognizable, universal human experience in literature are the ones who tend not to see the point of literature.

Good Practice #3: *Apply what you know about literature generally.*

Readers can comprehend and enjoy the classics better if they apply general literary methods of reading and analysis. We need to come to a classic (including the Bible) with the right literary expectations. This is a very broad subject, and I will cover only the basics.

First, we know that the subject of literature is universal human experience, rendered as concretely as possible. Part of the truth that literature imparts is truthfulness to reality and human experience. Literature shares this with the visual arts. If we do not know this, we are unlikely to see human experience in the literature that we read, and we will end up with an emaciated picture of literature as consisting of abstract ideas. History and the daily news tell us what *happened*; literature tells us what *happens*. It is not only a record of the author's time; it is also a record of our life and world. The classics as a whole are the human race's testimony to its own experience.

A second presupposition that we should make about a classic is that the form in which the work comes to us is important. Literary form is important to authors, so it needs to be important to us. The author of Ecclesiastes speaks for authors universally when he tells us that he arranged his material "with great care," and that he "sought to find words of delight" (12:9–10). He also signals his allegiance to the genre in which he writes when he speaks of the "proverbs" that he has weighed, studied, and arranged (v. 9). Literary authors lavish their attention on style and form, and they want us to admire the artifacts that they create for us.

C. S. Lewis has written with his usual good sense on this subject. Every work of literature, writes Lewis, "can be considered in two ways—as what the poet has to say, and as a *thing* which he *makes*." If readers concentrate unduly on content, "criticism becomes one-sided." And then Lewis delivers his famous verdict that "it is easy to forget that the man who writes a good love sonnet needs not only to be enamoured of a woman, but also to be enamoured of the Sonnet" (*A Preface to Paradise Lost*).

Novelist Joyce Cary's way of asserting that literary works embody a perspective was to say that "all writers . . . must have, to compose any kind of story, some picture of the world, and of what is right and wrong in that world" (*Art and Reality*).

A third presupposition that we should have in mind when reading a classic is that authors impose interpretive angles on the human experiences that they present. These interpretations can be formulated as ideas. With major works like epics, novels, and plays, the writer's interpretation of life expands into a worldview. A worldview is a mental and conceptual map of reality. A good methodology for reading "worldviewishly" is to regard the characters in literature as undertaking an experiment in living. On the basis of the outcome of that experiment, we can formulate a statement about life. A related piece of methodology is to assume that every work is an *example* that the author puts before us; the question to ask and answer is, What is this work an example *of*? For example, the story of Cain is an example of the destructive effects of unchecked evil in a person's life.

Good Practice #4: *Maintain a keen eye for the obvious*.

There is no doubt that the classics (especially the long masterworks) are complex works that appeal to us on many levels and in many ways. The things that we can do with them are inexhaustible. Authors want us to relish the details that they manage to pack into their works.

There is a potential problem with attentiveness to detail and traveling down the byways, though. Readers cannot sustain their interest in a work if the process of reading and analysis exceeds their tolerance for detail. After all, the classics are mainly works that we read as a leisure activity. C. S. Lewis criticized the sixteenth-century humanists for their inability "to respond to the central, obvious appeal of a great work" (*English Literature in the Sixteenth Century*). This is an extremely useful formula. One of the best questions that we can ask of a classic is, "What is the simple, obvious appeal of this work?" Answering the question can lead to good analysis of both the form and content of a work. Subsidiary questions are, what makes the subject matter good material for a story or poem, and what is most obviously appealing about the form of the work?

Good Practice #5: *Be aware that the classics did not escape the effects of the fall*.

We can almost depend on it that the classics will give us superior form and technique, and that the

C. S. Lewis is not the only literary critic who wants us not to overlook the simple, obvious aspect of a work. M. H. Abrams ended an essay that explored various approaches to Milton's poem *Lycidas* with the summary statement, "The necessary, though not sufficient, condition for a competent reader . . . remains what it has always been—a keen eye for the obvious" ("Five Types of *Lycidas*").

authors share the skill of their guild to be good observers of the human scene, combined with the ability to record that observation in words. These are simply the gifts that God has bestowed on writers. However, we should make no prejudgments about an author's worldview and moral vision simply because of these other superior skills. Our task as Christian readers is not to show *that* the classics state intellectual and moral truth but to ascertain *whether* they do.

The value structure and ideas that a classic embodies are known to us primarily from the subject matter that an author puts before us, combined with the perspective that the work itself reveals toward that subject matter. Every story or poem is a calculated strategy to get a reader to share the author's viewpoint. There is a latent persuasive element to every work of literature, and this is known by the technical name of the rhetoric of the work. We need to analyze this persuasive aspect and codify the results of it as themes or ideas about life.

The moral vision of a work is related to its value structure and worldview. Morality concerns people's relations to their fellow humans. It is easy to identify the moral vision of a work of literature. All we need to do is list the virtues (behavior that is offered for our approval) and vices (what is offered as negative behavior to avoid). Having codified the moral vision of a work, along with its ideas and worldview, we need to assess these things, and that leads to a final rule for reading the classics.

Good Practice #6: *Be yourself as a Christian reader.*

One of the four ingredients in the literary situation is the reader. Literary theory and criticism that elevate the role of the reader are known as reader-response (or reader-centered) criticism. Its dominance in the academy has long since passed, but there is a permanent legacy of the movement that Christians need to claim.

Reader-response criticism starts with something that can be proven, namely, that our personal responses are an important part of any reading experience. We cannot make these personal responses vanish, so we should bow to reality and acknowledge them. There is no such thing as a disembodied, objective experience of a work of literature. The further question becomes exactly what we should do with our personal responses and experiences of a work.

The wrong thing to do with them is to elevate them over the author and work. We do not have a right to make a work say what it does not say by bringing it into line with our responses. Our responses are self-revealing and may not tell us anything about the work. (On the other hand, our responses might be an index to what is in the work.) What we can say objectively is that certain groups of readers share a worldview, value structure, and moral system. These groups are called interpretive communities, a concept that evolved as reader-response criticism became established.

Christians are an interpretive community. They are not inherently better readers than other people. They are simply a group of readers who share a view of the authority of the Bible and who derive their beliefs from it. On the basis of the Bible, Christians have a shared doctrinal system and a common moral code. They also share a knowledge of the Bible, with the result that they are more likely than readers generally to see a bib-

In the twentieth century the preoccupation of poets and critics with the concreteness of literature produced the motto, "No ideas but in things." Poet Denise Levertov eventually sounded a caution that we not overlook the ideas in literature. She famously said, "'No ideas but in things' does not mean no ideas" (*The Poet in the World*).

lical presence in a work of literature and to credit it as a welcome dimension of the work.

Two things flow from the framework that Christians share as an interpretive community. One is that Christians have a common agenda of interests in regard to the classics. They are simply interested in the Christian and biblical dimensions of literature. Christians also ask how a given work accords with biblical truth and morality and how it deviates. At the same time, the passions of other interpretive communities may be of little interest to Christians (and vice versa). Christian readers naturally pick up on the Christian aspects of a work, just as members of other interpretive communities pick up on the things that interest them. Applied to reading and interpreting the classics, Christian readers should feel entirely free to follow their interests. When they do so, they are only doing what other interpretive communities do.

A second result of having a shared view of biblical authority and acceptance of Christian doctrine is that Christian readers have a standard by which to assess the truth or falseness of a work, as well as its morality or immorality. To make such an assessment is not something that Christians are simply free to do; it is something that they are obligated to do. Second Corinthians 10:5 speaks of bringing every thought captive to Christ. Weighing the truth claims of what we encounter in literature is a way of obeying that principle.

The general drift of being ourselves as Christian readers is to give us boldness to pursue the truth and remain committed to Christ when we read the classics. We should not allow ourselves to be intimidated by great authors or by other readers and literary critics. We have a right to be an

On the need not to be intimidated by a work simply because it is great, Francis Schaeffer offered the following advice: "As Christians, we must see that just because an artist—even a great artist—portrays a world view in writing or on canvas, it does not mean that we should automatically accept that world view. . . . The truth of a world view presented by an artist must be judged on separate grounds than artistic greatness" (*Art and the Bible*).

interpretive community. After all, everyone belongs to an interpretive community. All that is required of us is to be a responsible member of our community—knowing what the Bible and Christian doctrine and morality say, letting authors say what they really do say, and then exercising our prerogative of agreeing or disagreeing with them.

There is one more thing to say about being oneself as a Christian reader. It will have been evident from comments already made that I believe that we need to be slow to claim that works show a Christian allegiance when to others they do not show such an allegiance. We need to avoid baptizing works into the Christian camp simply because we love them. The situation is a little more complex than this, however. As Christian readers, we assimilate what we read in terms of our own Christian intuitions and values. To say that there is a Christian element in a work (or even to say that a given author or work *is* Christian) might be a comment on *how we assimilate a work* in keeping with our Christian orientation, even when we might not think that it was an author's intention. For example, in my thinking, Shakespeare has become a Christian writer (I say "become" because it is a view to which I gradually moved). I obviously cannot claim that for Homer, but at many points I see Christian congruences in *The Odyssey*, so I do not hesitate to say that Homer's elevation of home and family (for example) is a Christian element in the story, by which I mean that it accords with my Christian value structure.

On the need to be ourselves as Christian readers, Vincent Buckley has written, "It is the whole person who responds to a poem or novel; and if that person is a believing Christian, then it is a believing Christian who judges. . . . Literary criticism is as much a personal matter, as much the product of a personal sense of life and value as literature itself" (*Poetry and Morality*).

Chapter Summary

As Christian readers of the classics, we need to exercise balance. We need to expect the best of classics (especially in their formal excellence and the writers' skill in presenting life accurately), but we also need to be critical readers who assess the morality and truth claims of an author. We need to relish the simple appeal of a classic, while also being analytic in our attention to details and our assessment of a work's viewpoint. We need to value both the form and content of a classic.

CHAPTER 7

Christian Classics, Part 1

This chapter and the next two will explore the leading categories of literature that make up the domain of the classics. With the classics, even more than with literature generally, it is important to formulate accurate categories into which we place individual classics in our thinking. To cite a preliminary example, some classics have traditionally formed the school curriculum, others are prominent in culture generally, others belong to a specific subculture such as evangelical Christians, and some belong to our own personal lists of classics. We have different expectations for the various categories of classics.

A Taxonomy of Types of Literature

This unit is an introduction to the present chapter and the next two. The taxonomy that I am about to propose extends to all of literature and therefore to the classics as members of that category. The vantage point from which I survey the territory is that of a Christian reader.

Regarding Christian classics, British journalist Malcolm Muggeridge once wrote, "Books like *Resurrection* and *The Brothers Karamazov* give me an almost overpowering sense of how uniquely marvelous a Christian way of looking at life is, and a passionate desire to share it" (*Jesus Rediscovered*).

Christian literature is a category that Christian readers immediately claim as a special possession. It begins with the Bible, which provides a good paradigm for defining the entire category. Within the realm of Christian literature, there are further subcategories, which I will define shortly. Even though Christians should read much in addition to the literature of the faith, I believe that Christian readers should especially resonate with the literature of Zion (metaphorically speaking), and I am always perplexed when Christians find their chief literary excitement in non-Christian literature. In the overall canon of Western classics, Christian classics comprise approximately half of the material. This is true because Christianity was the dominant belief system in the West for seventeen centuries.

The other half of the realms of gold that we call the classics is non-Christian literature. A more manageable label is "secular," and I will use that term in this guide, even though there is a certain inaccuracy about the term because, strictly speaking, *secular* means "without a religious basis." Many non-Christian writers are religious in their outlook. With secular literature too there are subcategories. For example, it is common for Christians to label the literature of classical antiquity (Greco-Roman culture) *pagan*, to denote that it was pre-Christian and therefore independent of Christian influence. But it is obvious that classical cultures were thoroughly religious, so that the word *pagan* carries connotations of classical religion and thereby avoids the wrong associations of the word *secular*.

When we come to secular or non-Christian literature that began in the Christian era, we find a sliding scale. Closest to the Christian camp is literature that makes no overt commitment to the Christian faith (though it may make use of the Bible) but is congruent with the Christian faith and may even have been written by a Christian. Then as we move down the continuum, we find literature that seems less and less connected to the Christian faith but can still be claimed as congruent with the beliefs and morality of a Christian reader. To some degree it is ideologically neutral—not overtly Christian but easily assimilated into a Christian worldview. At the far end of the continuum we find literature that either by design or by intellectual or moral allegiance is hostile to Christianity. Here Christian readers find themselves in an adversarial stance to what they read.

Types of Christian Literature

Christian literature is identifiable chiefly but not only by its content. Literary form per se does not have a religious or intellectual allegiance. We can, however, say that certain aspects of literary form originally came from the Christian tradition and are therefore a Christian element in a work, even when they appear in a secular work. The most obvious example is allusions to the Bible, or even an author's taking story material or content from the Bible. Alternatively, a writer might write in a biblical genre such as the praise psalm or apocalyptic writing. A third formal element that has been important throughout English and American literature consists of a writer's using vocabulary or imagery from the Bible or the Christian tradition, even if that vocabulary or imagery is used for new purposes. In all of these cases, the right terminology to use is that a given work *intersects with the*

Christian faith, even though we might not consider the work as a whole a Christian work of literature.

The ultimate standard for calling a work Christian is the intellectual content of a work. A *Christian* literary work is one in which the author asserts a Christian allegiance at the level of ideas and morality. Whether the writer personally embraces that Christian content is not directly relevant and may be impossible to know. What matters is what the work itself asserts. Having said that, genuinely Christian writers tend overwhelmingly to make their allegiance clear, so that the work becomes a personal testimony of the author's faith.

Within the realm of Christian classics, an important dichotomy emerges between (1) subject matter and (2) the perspective that a writer takes toward that subject. Some Christian literature takes specifically spiritual experience as its subject matter. An obvious example is devotional poetry, or an explicitly Christian work like Milton's *Paradise Lost*. In other Christian literature it is not the subject matter that is religious but the perspective that the author brings to bear on the subject. For example, Gerard Manley Hopkins's poem "God's Grandeur" takes as its subject matter something on which many Romantic poets had written before, namely, rapture over the beauty and freshness of nature. In itself, that subject might be said to be neutral or "secular." The Christian aspect of Hopkins's poem is the perspective by which the poet asserts that the permanent freshness of nature is attributable to God and that it declares the greatness of God (as hinted in the title—"God's Grandeur").

One more piece of taxonomy is important. In

terms of theme and worldview, we can picture all of literature as made up of two overlapping circles (Diagram 7.1). One of the circles represents Christian belief and morality. The other circle represents other religious and philosophical systems. The overlapping part of the diagram represents *inclusively* Christian material that includes Christianity and other religious or philosophical systems. The part of the Christian circle that falls outside the overlapping area is *exclusively* Christian content. It excludes or separates Christian belief from other religions. The part of the circle that falls outside of the overlapping area represents non-Christian and potentially anti-Christian material.

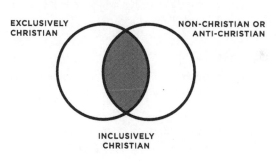

EXCLUSIVELY CHRISTIAN

NON-CHRISTIAN OR ANTI-CHRISTIAN

INCLUSIVELY CHRISTIAN

Diagram 7.1

Christian authors have diverged on the question of what constitutes the proper subject matter of their writing. One strand of thinking is represented by seventeenth-century poet George Herbert, who claimed that "God must have my best, even all I had" ("The Forerunners"). For Herbert, this meant writing on explicitly Christian subject matter, such as God, Christian doctrine, events in the yearly church calendar like Christmas and Easter, and specifically spiritual experiences like forgiveness and salvation.

There is no valid reason for disparaging what is inclusively Christian in a work of literature. Something is no less Christian for being a viewpoint that adherents of other religions also believe. One result of this is that Christian readers are free to find their faith strewn more widely in the fields of imaginative literature than a narrow definition of Christian literature would allow. We need to draw the line somewhere, of course, but we can in good conscience see the Christian faith in much of our reading of the classics. Until "political correctness" became the dominant force in education and culture, the classics represented a common ground where Christians and non-Christians could meet, free from the divisiveness of politically correct liberalism. Christians lost a lot when that common ground was taken from them.

I will also say by way of personal testimony that the classics have been a very important source of spiritual input in my life. This is partly a comment on how I assimilate what I read and is not an automatic aspect of the literature involved. We need to avoid confusing literary experience with religious or spiritual experience, but we should not exclude literary experience from the spiritual life when for us personally it is a religious as well as an artistic experience.

Bible Reading as a Model

In the remainder of this chapter I will explore how to read a Christian classic. A good entry into the subject is to ask how we read the Bible (the greatest classic) and what happens when we read it. There is one big difference between reading the Bible and reading the classics: the Bible is without error and is not on trial. It is our authority and not a book whose truth claims we need to assess. Its role for us as we read other classics is that of a standard by which we weigh their themes and moral vision. But in other ways our reading of the Bible provides good answers to the question of how we should read a Christian classic.

The first thing we can say about Bible reading is that, as Christians, we begin with the liberating knowledge that we will be nurtured by what we are about to read. These are the words of life, and we can find that exhilarating. Related to that,

Another view that Christian writers have adopted regarding literary subject matter is that the Christian element consists not of subject matter but of the interpretive angle that the writer takes toward a given human experience, whatever it might be. Flannery O'Connor is in this camp when she writes that a Catholic novel is not necessarily identifiable by its subject matter "but simply that . . . the truth as Christians know it has been used as a light to see the world by" (*Mystery and Manners*).

we know that the reading of the Bible is more than a purely literary experience. It is not less than that, but it is more. We know with our minds that reading literature of any kind is valuable to us as a potential source of insight into human experience, but often we need to work hard to make sure that we are gaining and appropriating that insight. When we read the Bible, we are completely aware that this is the source of light for daily living. When we read a Christian classic, we experience something similar.

A second way in which the Bible serves as a model stems from its literary nature. The Bible gives us a definition of a Christian classic. It is not all equally literary, and this should keep us from overstating the case for the importance of literature (as though nonliterary forms of writing are inferior). But the Bible is predominantly literary. It overwhelmingly presents human experience in the concrete form of character, events, settings, and images. As a result, when we sit down to read a Christian classic, we are freed from anxiety about the worthiness of what we are about to do. Additionally, the Bible is a book overflowing with literary form and technique. If we can give ourselves to literary form when reading the Bible, we can do it with other Christian classics.

By meeting all the criteria of being literary, the Bible shows us that before a work can be a Christian classic, it needs to be a classic. It needs to meet ordinary criteria of literary excellence. There is a place for expository religious writing, but a work of literature needs to be literary. Religious content by itself does not produce a Christian classic.

The example of the Bible also extends the range of subject matter that we can regard as worthy of a Christian classic. Because we ordinarily limit our Bible reading to the most overtly spiritual sections, we tend to have a somewhat unrealistic picture of what all is in the Bible. If we read the entire Bible, we are amazed at how much non-religious content there is—bodily ailments and hygiene in the Pentateuch, military history in the chronicles, court history in those same books, and detailed pictures of social life in the Old Testament prophetic books. If this seemingly "secular" content is in the Bible, we need not be uptight when we find it in the Christian classics.

The example of the Bible also sheds light on the issue of inclusively Christian literature versus exclusively Christian literature. Overall, the Bible views all of human experience from a God-centered and religious viewpoint. We should pause on the formula "all of human experience." The Bible covers pretty much all of life, not only specifically spiritual experiences like prayer and forgiveness of sin and good and evil, but also national history, harvest, sunrise, and losing an axe in a body of water. To this we can add the concept of inclusively Christian literature in the Bible.

While most of the Bible views human experience in an explicitly Christian light, some of it does not. The Song of Solomon is an anthology of love lyrics without religious references. The book of Esther mentions religious practices such as prayer and fasting, but it does not attribute the events of the story to God, who is not named. Many of the proverbs in the Old Testament book by that name belong to the phenomenon of international wisdom literature of the time and portray common wisdom for everyday living, not specifically spiritual issues. If we find this latitude in the

Bible, we should not be uneasy when we find it in the Christian classics.

Reading Christian Classics

With these thoughts about reading the Bible in our awareness, we are in a good position to explore the dimensions of reading Christian classics. A good framework to bring into the discussion is the twofold purpose of literature. Writing two decades before the birth of Christ, the Roman poet Horace bequeathed a formula that has stood the test of time. Horace said that literature combines what is useful (*utile*) with what is sweet (*dulci*) or delightful (*The Art of Poetry*). Variants have reverberated through the centuries of literary theory—teach and delight, truth and delight, wisdom and pleasure. These are the purposes of literature—the things that a writer aspires to put into a work and the effects that a reader experiences when reading it.

We can legitimately bring both of these expectations to the reading of a Christian classic. There is absolutely no reason to waive the usual criterion of pleasure and enjoyment when we read Christian classics (including the Bible). Literature is an art form. There is a category known as didactic literature ("having the intention to teach"), and I do not want to rule it out entirely, but a true classic is something that we read for the full range of literary rewards and not as we read a book of information.

The best words by which to identify the other purpose of literature (what Horace called *utile* or "useful") are *edification*, *edify*, and *edifying*. Edification includes the idea of imparting truth, but it goes beyond that to mean being uplifted

Francis Schaeffer cast his lot with the view that Christian art consists not of religious subject matter but instead the Christian perspective that is brought to bear on any subject: "*Christian art is by no means always religious art, that is, art which deals with religious themes.* Consider God the Creator. Is God's creation totally involved with religious subjects? . . . If God made the flowers, they are worth painting and writing about. . . . If God made the ocean, indeed it's worth writing poetry about" (*Art and the Bible*).

by what we have heard or read. Christian classics enrich our mind and elevate our soul. Matthew Arnold's formula (Preface to *Poems*) about poetry can be applied to Christian classics: they "inspirit and rejoice" our heart and mind. We are improved or uplifted by the experience. To quote again a definition of a classic that appears earlier in this book, when we are edified by a classic we feel that "we are not the same men and women we were when we began it" (Sheldon Sacks, *Fiction and the Shape of Belief*).

I want to push this in an affective or emotional direction as well. Many enthusiasts for literature have described a certain state of mind, soul, and emotion that characterizes our best literary experiences. I would not limit this experience to Christian classics, but I think that it is preeminently true of reading the Christian classics, including the Bible. Here are specimen statements:

- In a description of the effects produced by Christian poetry, John Milton said that such poetry is "of such power, beside [along with] the power of a pulpit, to . . . allay the perturbations of the mind, and set the affections [the old word for emotions] in right tune" (*The Reason of Church Government*).
- Matthew Arnold praised the effects of poetry in a statement that I am here applying to a Christian's assimilation of a Christian classic: poetry has "the power of so dealing with things as to awaken in us a wonderfully full, new, and intimate sense of them, and of our relations with them. When this sense is awakened in us . . . we feel ourselves to be in contact with the essential nature of those objects, to be

The main text of this chapter applies quotations from Milton, Arnold, and Shelley to the effects of reading Christian classics. Sven Birkerts provides one more quotation. In making the point that what readers often seek is not the specific content of a literary work but the effects of "the reading state." Birkerts defines this reading state as follows: "In this condition, when all is clear and right . . . I feel a connectedness that cannot be duplicated." This time of reading, adds Birkerts, "is not the world's time, but the soul's" ("The Woman in the Garden").

no longer bewildered and oppressed by them, but to have their secret, and to be in harmony with them; and this feeling calms and satisfies us as no other can" (*Essays in Criticism*).

- Romantic poet Percy Shelley, in his *Defense of Poetry*, also made a comment about the effects of poetry that I am applying specifically to our reading of Christian classics: "The good affections [emotions] are strengthened, . . . and an exalted calm is prolonged."

Obviously I am making very large claims for the beneficial effects of reading the Christian classics. Ordinary literature can produce the same effects, but not with the same regularity and richness as Christians classics give us.

We should not overstate the case for Christian classics. Even they did not escape the effects of the fall. Just as not every sermon that we hear or Christian book that we read strikes as true in every respect, not every Christian classic "gets it right" according to our understanding of Christian belief. Christian classics require the same process of assessment that we apply to other literature. The Bible is the standard by which such a judgment is determined. Usually such weighing of the assertions of a Christian author by biblical truth and morality results in our affirming the accuracy of the vision. Conversely, relatively rarely do we decide that a Christian author has missed the mark. This is true because overwhelmingly the Christian classics reside in the realm of what has become known as "mere Christianity"—the universal aspects of the Christian faith that all Christians can affirm.

"Throughout the centuries certain books have had a tremendous influence on Christians across traditions and cultures. The ideas expressed in these seminal works have shaped the history not only of Christianity but also the world" (publisher's blurb for *25 Books Every Christian Should Read*).

Chapter Summary

Christian classics are one of God's greatest gifts to the human race. They rise to the status of being classics by virtue of their literary excellence; they belong to the category of Christian classic because their worldview and intellectual allegiance adhere to Christian doctrine. Christian classics comprise a range of subcategories, and although they have unique ability to edify a Christian reader, they nonetheless need to be scrutinized by the light of the Bible.

CHAPTER 8

Christian Classics, Part 2

The preceding chapter contains the thoughts that I consider to be primary in regard to Christian literary classics. This chapter takes up specialized topics in regard to Christian classics.

"Crossover" Classics

Every field has its classics. There are sports classics and classic bloopers. In a field like literature, some classics are legitimately claimed by other disciplines as well. These are called *crossover books*. A commonly accepted example is books that appeal to both children and adults. Another category is books that appeal to both Christian and secular markets.

The category "Christian classic" is a crossover category. Classics like Augustine's *Confessions* or Bunyan's *Pilgrim's Progress* are taught in both literature courses and theology courses, and sometimes in writing courses devoted to the genre of autobiography or memoir writing.

A further twist is that to the general public, the label *Christian classic* does not conjure up literary works at all. If one enters "Christian classics" into an online search engine, what comes up are theological and devotional books such as Thomas à Kempis's *The Imitation of Christ* and C. S. Lewis's *Mere Christianity* and A. W. Tozer's *The Pursuit of God*. We do not need to drop the literary label of *Christian classics*, but we need to be aware of possible misunderstandings.

The Alleged Christian Classic

Among the special situations that arise in regard to Christian literary classics is one in which people attach the label of *Christian classic* to a work that we personally do not find to be Christian in nature. Of course there is no objective, infallible way of assessing whether a work meets the criteria for being Christian. This means that we are left with subjective judgments.

We need to be prepared for disagreements and not be swept off our feet by them. An alternate title for this unit might have been "On Having the Courage of Your Own Convictions." We cannot read very far in published literary criticism before we discover that virtually all works of literature have been interpreted in opposing ways. Such variability exists right within the interpretive community of Christian readers and critics.

For most Christian classics, there is a consensus among both scholars and general readers that they are Christian in orientation (even though readers might disagree about the exact nature of their Christian perspective). But for a few works

A university professor of literature named Joseph Summers long ago sounded the following note of caution about being overly zealous to pin the *Christian* label on authors and works: "Many of the most talented writers have been either extremely vague about religious issues or have been consciously non-Christian or anti-Christian. . . . However fashionable, or even artistically successful, a work may be, . . . we should not fool ourselves into thinking that all of our responses or 'likings' are inevitably religious or Christian. . . . We betray [Christian standards] . . . if we try to present popular non-Christian works as 'essentially Christian' merely because we want Christianity, too, to be popular" ("Christian Literary Scholars").

and authors, there is disagreement about the accuracy of calling them *Christian*. Was the English Romantic poet William Blake a Christian writer? I recall a time when opinion within my own English department was divided on that question. Is Emily Dickinson's poetry Christian in its intellectual allegiance? The claim is sometimes made. The current trend is so strong to question Christian interpretations that it is hard to imagine that half a century ago, the situation was the reverse of that. It is still common in Christian circles to claim that favorite authors and works are Christian even in doubtful situations.

Christian readers should have the courage to reach their own decisions in regard to disputed Christian classics. If we believe that a work or author measures up to our definition of Christianity, we should not be intimidated by people who do not believe the work is Christian (see the next section for more on this). On the other side, we should avoid being swayed by claims for a Christian allegiance in works or authors that seem to us not to measure up.

The Christianized Secular Text

A Christian classic carries its Christian meanings within itself and does not require us to place it into a context to determine its Christian allegiance. Often, though, additional meanings emerge when we do evoke a context. For example, there are some Christian classics that were intended by their authors to serve the polemical or argumentative purpose of refuting a non-Christian tradition. The technical term for this is *intertext*—a situation in which a work is designed as an interaction with an already-existing text or body of literature in

John Steadman writes as follows about Milton's Christianizing of the classical tradition in *Paradise Lost*: "For the praise of men he substituted the glory of God. . . . Instead of the physical warfare of secular polities, he described the moral conflict of spiritual societies. Instead of celebrating heroic exploits, he stressed their imperfections. . . . Undermining the established epic tradition by destroying its ethical foundations, *Paradise Lost* is at once both epic and counter epic. If it imitates the established models of heroic poetry, it also refutes them" (*Milton and the Renaissance Hero*).

such a way that the meaning of the enterprise can be viewed as existing *between* the two texts. The dialogue or refutation is an important part of the meaning.

Milton's *Paradise Lost* is the best example. Milton participated in a tradition that began relatively early in the Middle Ages to determine how the Christian faith related to the classical tradition in which authors and readers had been educated. There is evidence within *Paradise Lost* that Milton intended his epic to refute the epic tradition that he inherited, not at the level of epic form but at the level of ideas and values.

The classical epic tradition was humanistic in orientation. Its heroes were not irreligious, nor were the gods absent from the action, but the heroes achieved their feats mainly through human self-reliance. The goals that these heroes pursued were earthly fame, success, and empire. The epic feat was winning a battle, and it was axiomatic in this tradition that the crucial events of history happened on the battlefield.

Milton introduces aspects of this into his poem only to expose their deficiency. For example, he introduces a boastful warrior—Satan—only to show how evil he is. Overall, Milton's anti-epic strategy (as it is now regularly called) consisted of replacing the epic warrior as hero with the Christian saint as hero, and replacing military values with pastoral and domestic values. Milton made the garden rather than the battlefield the scene of his epic feat. And what is that feat? Eating an apple—not an act of glory but of shame, thereby exploding classical and humanistic illusions of human greatness. The setting for the epic feat was

According to T. J. B. Spencer, Milton wrote *Paradise Lost* with a "sense of rivalry with the poets of the past, instead of a sense of merely inheriting a great tradition. . . . It is now at last obvious what *Paradise Lost* is. It is the anti-epic. Wherever we turn we find the traditional epic values inverted" in a Christian direction ("*Paradise Lost*: The Anti-Epic").

not the battlefield but the human soul, and it was not a physical act but a spiritual one.

Epics always represent the author's verdict on what constitutes heroic (exemplary) action. Homer assumed that human self-exertion and earthly success constitute heroic action. Milton's version of heroic action is seen in Adam and Eve's virtuous life in Paradise and consists of devotion to God, perfect married companionship, harmony with nature, contentedness, and living the simple life. These virtues are virtually the opposite of the values of classical epic.

The moment of epiphany toward which *Paradise Lost* moves comes late in the poem as Adam responds to the vision of future history that Michael has given him. The vision is followed by Adam's summary statement of what he has learned, and this is Milton's new and Christianized epic norm. It consists of coming to trust in Christ as Savior.

The foregoing is a very brief account of what it means that Milton Christianized the classical tradition. *Paradise Lost* can be called a Christianized classical text.

I will briefly mention two other examples of a writer's Christianizing an existing tradition. There can be no doubt that Shakespeare was familiar with classical tragedies and with Aristotle's ideas about tragedy as formulated in his *Poetics*. The template on which Shakespeare composed plays like *Macbeth* and *King Lear* was classical tragedy. But Shakespeare wrote in a Christian era, and whether by design or unconsciously (simply because of the Christian culture in which he wrote), Shakespeare's tragedies run counter to several important premises of Greek tragedy. Greek tragedy

Often the rehabilitation of a misrepresented Christian classic begins with encountering a piece of published criticism that sets the compass in the right direction. For Shakespeare's *The Merchant of Venice*, a landmark essay, "Biblical Allusion and Allegory in *The Merchant of Venice*" (often reprinted), by Barbara Lewalski can fill that role. Lewalski analyzes the entire play to show how the action affirms a Christian view of mercy and redemption. The trial scene enacts the theological debate of justice versus mercy. The Jew Shylock is forced to see that he cannot achieve his goal by means of the law. As in Christian theology, mercy achieves what the law cannot.

is ultimately the tragedy of fate, whereas Shakespeare's tragedies follow the Christian paradigm of placing the responsibility for evil action on the tragic hero's tragic flaw of character. Tragic heroes in the classical tragedy are victims of ignorance, whereas those in Shakespeare are clear-sighted about what they should do and how their actions violate that moral standard. It is entirely plausible to read Shakespearean tragedy as a revision of classical tragedy.

If we fast-forward nearly three centuries, we come to another intertext with Nathaniel Hawthorne's *The Scarlet Letter*. Hawthorne lived in Massachusetts alongside such Romantics as Henry David Thoreau and Ralph Waldo Emerson. He was bombarded with Romantic ideas about feeling and nature. He introduced the Romantic ideals into his masterwork in the form of Hester. But he also put a Christian worldview into his book, and after letting the two worldviews fight it out, Hawthorne ends by siding with the Christian worldview. In fact, he handles the debate between Hester and Dimmesdale in such a way as to make the Christian conclusion of his story an obvious refutation of Romanticism. *The Scarlet Letter* is thus a Christianized Romantic text.

Once alerted to the phenomenon of a Christian work that challenges an existing tradition, we will find it scattered throughout English and American literature. The model actually began with the Bible. Psalm 29, the song of the thunderstorm, is modeled on a surrounding pagan myth of Baal. The poem repeats all the standard motifs, but the poet substitutes God for Baal and thereby conducts an argument against paganism. The Christ hymn at the beginning of the Gospel of

There is an abundance of Christian interpretations of *The Scarlet Letter*. The problem is that they are suppressed in the classroom. Randall Stewart, in his book *American Literature and Christian Doctrine*, was an early exponent of the view that *The Scarlet Letter* is a Christian classic: "Hester is not the protagonist, the chief actor, and the tragedy of *The Scarlet Letter* is not her tragedy but Arthur's. He is the persecuted one, the tempted one. . . . His public confession is one of the noblest climaxes of tragic literature. . . . The confession was decisive. Its function in the novel is to resolve the action. It turned the scales in the great debate, though Hester, romantic heretic to the end, remained unconvinced, impenitent, unredeemed."

John (1:1–18) imitates a hymn to Zeus that Greeks had sung for several centuries, but it Christianizes the hymn by ascribing praise to Christ instead of Zeus.

The Unacknowledged Christian Classic

I come finally to the vexing phenomenon of the unrecognized Christian classic—a work that we believe to be Christian but that the secular world (and some Christian scholars as well) treat as a non-Christian or even anti-Christian work. I have had a small side-career as a rehabilitator of these misrepresented Christian classics, and I offer what I hope will be helpful strategies for anyone who wishes to follow in my footsteps.

Examples of unacknowledged or misrepresented Christian classics that have been important in my scholarly life include Nathaniel Hawthorne's *The Scarlet Letter*, Christopher Marlowe's *Doctor Faustus*, Shakespeare's *The Merchant of Venice*, Leo Tolstoy's *The Death of Ivan Ilych* (which a published source told me was a humanistic rather than Christian work), and that Shakespeare is a Christian writer. Instead of repeating the specifics of my views on these (some of which are the subject of individual books in my Crossway series of Christian Guides to the Classics), I will outline the typical paradigm that has unfolded in each case.

Often the starting point for my eventual reclamation of a work or author began in a graduate school classroom, though sometimes the genesis has been a piece of published literary criticism. If I had attended a secular college, probably the starting point would have been an undergraduate literature course. In any case, the process began with what seemed to be a deliberate attempt to suppress

In most classrooms, *The Scarlet Letter* is interpreted as extolling Romanticism and denouncing Christianity. But if one reads enough criticism, Christian interpretations of Hawthorne's masterpiece become a small library. Here are specimen statements: "The last scene on the scaffold is a complete vision of salvation" (W. Stacy Johnson, "Sin and Salvation in Hawthorne"). "The final section of *The Scarlet Letter* shows Dimmesdale, apparently doomed to perdition, spectacularly saved by God's grace" (Darrel Abel, *The Moral Picturesque*).

the Christian element in a work, sometimes as a larger disparagement of the Christian faith.

I would not have chafed under the way in which the work was mishandled in the classroom if my intuitions had not already convinced me that the work or author was Christian in orientation. In the typical pattern, as I kept reading published scholarship, I would eventually uncover a cloud of witnesses who confirmed my intuitions about the Christian allegiance of the work or author. I have never been a lone voice in reclaiming misrepresented Christian classics. Usually the older criticism helped me more than recent criticism, but this has not been uniformly true. When I published my own Christian interpretations of unacknowledged Christian classics, I usually received a gratifying abundance of correspondence from like-minded readers. With my intuitions confirmed by published criticism, I would go back to the text with renewed vigor and find more and more Christian elements in the work.

With the foregoing paradigm before us, I offer four principles that might lift the drooping hands of readers who have found themselves embattled because Christian classics are misrepresented.

1. Do not be intimidated by the pronouncements of a non-Christian or secular culture or viewpoint (even if that viewpoint is urged upon you by a fellow Christian).

2. Operate on the premise that if you search thoroughly enough, you will find published scholarship to confirm you in your interpretation.

3. If you are sure that your Christian interpretation is supported by the text,

Leo Kirschbaum had a courageous career in setting the record straight about the Christian element in Shakespeare's *The Merchant of Venice* and Christopher Marlowe's *Doctor Faustus*. He struck a blow for truth with the following statement: "Marlowe's Faustus has so often been described by modern critics as a superman, reaching out for infinite knowledge and ineffable beauty, as an individual whom we ought proudly to esteem as representative of aspiring humanity, that one almost hesitates to disagree with this well-nigh universal opinion. Yet, surprisingly, it is unsupported by the play itself. . . . Let us see the play in the terms of the basic Christian values it preaches" ("Religious Values in *Doctor Faustus*").

keep digging for more and more data
to confirm your interpretation.
4. Share the good news. Accept the rehabilitation of the work as a personal
mission.

Chapter Summary

Christian classics are a paradox. Reading them can
be an oasis in life. Reading them confirms us and
refreshes us. But they are not always represented
accurately. We can let our guard down in personal
reading of them as Christian classics, but when we
enter the public arena, we may need to enter into a
debate regarding them.

CHAPTER 9

Secular Classics

What I call a secular work is a non-Christian work
that does not explicitly endorse a Christian view
of reality. It is a term of convenience that I have
chosen over the label "non-Christian," which is a
bit unwieldy. But in using the word *secular* in this
way, I need to modify its dictionary definition to
include the possibility of a religious (though non-
Christian) viewpoint, whereas technically the
word implies that the subject being discussed is
void of religious belief.

The Landscape

The body of literature that I discuss in this chapter encompasses a range of literature and is not as
monolithic as the chapter title might suggest. At

one end of the literary continuum as a whole, we find Christian literature that not only intersects with the Bible and Christian belief but endorses them (Diagram 9.1). This is where we find Christian classics (as discussed in the two preceding chapters). Next, we find a category of literature that stops short of endorsing an explicitly Christian viewpoint but that is not hostile to it or necessarily an alternative to it. Christianity is simply absent from the worldview by way of explicit reference.

LITERATURE OF
Christian Affirmation

LITERATURE OF
Clarification or
Common Humanity

LITERATURE OF
Unbelief

Diagram 9.1

Even within this category we find a certain range. One subcategory is literature that stops short of signaling Christian commitment but that is entirely congruent with Christian belief and morality. In fact, the author may have been a Christian. The work may include biblical allusions, use the Bible as a model, and refer to Christian beliefs or texts. I have already labeled such literature "inclusively Christian," meaning that the viewpoint includes Christianity and other religious or ethical traditions. Obviously such a work is a crossover work that is partly Christian and partly non-Christian (but not anti-Christian).

Much of the literature that I read and teach falls into this category. Often it nurtures my soul in the same ways that Christian literature does. I use two labels to identify this body of literature. One is *the literature of common humanity*. This literature speaks to us as members of the human

"Abelard asked a very foolish question when he asked: 'What has Horace to do with the Psalter, Virgil with the Gospel, Cicero with the Apostle?' The answer is simply that Horace, Virgil, and Cicero clarify the human situation to which the salvation of God is addressed. . . . Christian faith addresses itself to the very situation which literature clarifies, examines, and makes in some limited measure manageable" (Roland M. Frye, *Perspective on Man*).

race and can serve as a bond between us and the human community. I also call this body of literature *the literature of clarification*. It does not affirm a Christian view of life, but it clarifies the human situation to which the Christian faith speaks. Often we can make a slightly stronger claim: this literature does not expound Christian doctrine but may point to it.

The other half of the middle part of the literary continuum takes a step away from Christianity by setting up a degree of dissonance with it. It is not at the far end of the continuum where we find literature that contradicts Christianity, but it emerges in our thinking as an alternative to Christianity. This literature belongs to the literature of common humanity and clarification, but we would hesitate to call it inclusively Christian.

Then, without a clear line of demarcation, we find ourselves at the far end of the continuum where we are presented with something that is not simply different from the Christian viewpoint but something that contradicts it. It may *explicitly* reject the Christian viewpoint. Even if it stops short of overt rejection of Christianity, as Christian readers we are fully aware that we are being given a rival viewpoint to our own. I call this *the literature of unbelief*. I will note in passing that whereas in the previous chapter I explored the phenomenon of the Christianized secular text, in the literature of unbelief it is not uncommon to find authors who secularize the Christian tradition in a similar manner, replying to it and refuting it.

Having drawn certain boundaries, I will nonetheless consider the non-Christian categories as a single group as I now explore why and how we should read secular classics. Our strategies of reading and interpreting are essentially the same with all the categories (inclusively Christian, the literature of common humanity and clarification, and the literature of unbelief), even though the application of the principles is slightly different and our experience of the respective categories might vary.

Why Secular Literature Can Be Good for Us

I have decided to answer the question of why Christians should read secular classics—the value that they hold—before I offer a methodology for reading them. Unless we agree that secular classics can enrich our lives, it is superfluous to talk about how to read them.

One of the values that secular classics offer us is implicit in my labels *the literature of common humanity* and *the literature of clarification*. The subject of literature is human experience. Literature overwhelmingly "delivers the goods" in putting us in touch with bedrock human experience. Flannery O'Connor said that the writer "should never be ashamed of staring" at life (*Mystery and Manners*). The same is true of readers. One of the functions of authors is "to *stare*, to *look* at the created world, and to lure the rest of us into a similar act of contemplation" (Nathan A. Scott, *Modern Literature and the Religious Frontier*). As we stare at human experience, we come to understand it. Literature gives us knowledge in the form of right seeing, and this applies to secular literature too.

Christian and secular classics both give us this form of knowledge, but the clarifying power of literature (its focus on human experience) assumes a larger proportion of the take-away value when we read secular literature. We do not have

The following statement about painters is also true of literary authors: "Because a painter is not a Christian, that does not mean that his paintings cannot be enjoyed or even imitated by Christians. To be sure any thematic content must be scrutinized very critically through the lens of Scripture, but art as art is essentially neutral. . . . Was the person who made my shoes or cooked for me in a restaurant a Christian? . . . Even if he or she was not a Christian, I am not harmed spiritually by my clothing or my meal" (Gene Edward Veith Jr., *The Gift of Art*).

our souls nurtured in the same way that we do when we read Christian literature, so truthfulness to human experience and clarification of life loom larger as the things that occupy us.

This clarification of life extends in two directions. It is a truism that literature is *a mirror* in which we see ourselves. At a 1924 commemorative ceremony at the tomb of Renaissance Flemish painter Pieter Brueghel, a speaker said, "In your work are reflected ... our joys and our sorrows, our strengths and our weaknesses. . . . You are our mirror. . . . To know what we are, we have only to thumb through the book of your art, and we can know ourselves" (quoted in Bob Claessens, *Pieter Brueghel*).

But literature is not only a mirror; it is also *a window* to the world. There is a communal aspect to our literary experiences as we look beyond ourselves to the experiences of others. Reading secular literature can help us form a bond with the human race, and sometimes this is even truer when we read the literature of unbelief. Literature highlights the human condition to which the Christian faith speaks. Often we feel this more strongly when we know that we are being addressed by an unbelieving author who gives testimony to a viewpoint or experience that we do not know directly.

Finally, as already hinted, secular classics offer the values that I ascribed to all classics earlier in this book. All classics put us in touch with bedrock human experience. All of them give us an optimum of literary form and beauty. All of them embody important ideas that can serve as a catalyst to our own thinking about the great issues of life. All of them open a doorway to the past. If we are convinced of the benefits of reading the classics

John Calvin wrote the following about common grace: "To charge the human intellect with perpetual blindness, then, and to leave it no intelligence whatever is repugnant not only to the Word of God but common sense. For we see grafted into the mind of man a desire to investigate truth. . . . When we read secular writers and find an admirable light of truth in them, it should remind us that the human mind, fallen and perverted as it is from its original integrity, is still clothed and adorned with God's excellent gifts" (*Institutes*).

in general, the values of secular classics are self-evident, even though we experience those values in a different way from when we read a Christian classic.

How Not to Read a Secular Classic

I will begin by addressing pitfalls into which we can easily fall as Christian readers of secular classics. The first is the error of avoidance. In view of the values that secular classics can provide, to avoid them represents a missed opportunity. Missed opportunities are a terrible waste. Tony Reinke lists a number of impeccable "benefits of reading non-Christian books" (*Lit: A Christian Guide to Reading Books*) that should convince us of the need to find space for secular classics in our lives.

A second way not to read secular classics is to read with what scholars call "a hermeneutic of suspicion"—looking for trouble at every turn. To read with suspicion means to presume that an author "got it wrong" and that the only possible function of a book is to prompt us to disagree with it. When we read with this type of suspicion, we begin from a stance of hostility and are not open to receive something positive. This is not to say that we should not be wary and on guard, but we can be alert without assuming that an author or work is our opponent on every count.

A third error is the exact opposite of the second. It consists of giving automatic preference to non-Christian writers, on the assumption that they can be trusted to be more truthful than Christian writers, at least in the portrayal of human experience. It is no doubt true that unbelieving authors understand certain aspects of unregenerate experience better than Christians usually do. But

Augustine famously compared gleaning truth from secular writers to the Israelites' spoiling the Egyptians when they fled from Egypt: if pagan thinkers "have said anything that is true and in harmony with our faith, we are not only not to shrink from it, but to claim it for our own use from those who have unlawful possession of it. For, as the Egyptians had . . . vessels and ornaments of gold and silver, and garments, which the same people when going out of Egypt appropriated for themselves, designing them for a better use," we can do the same today in regard to pagan culture (*On Christian Doctrine*).

through the years I have regularly encountered the unwarranted sentiment that non-Christian authors or scholars or universities somehow rank higher than Christian ones. It is simply untrue.

How to Read a Secular Classic

My first piece of advice may surprise some of my readers, but it is a settled conviction based on years of experience. To read secular classics we need to *be thoroughly convinced of the doctrine of common grace.* This doctrine is explicitly (though not abundantly) stated in the Bible and has been championed especially by the Reformed or Calvinistic tradition. The doctrine of common grace holds that God endows all people, Christian and non-Christian alike, with a capacity for the true, the good, and the beautiful. It lies beyond my purpose here to adduce the biblical data on which this doctrine is based, so I will allow John Calvin to give a summary of it: "The mind of man, though fallen and perverted from its wholeness, is nevertheless clothed and ornamented with God's excellent gifts. . . . All truth is from God; and consequently, if wicked men have said anything that is true and just, we ought not to reject it; for it has come from God" (*Institutes* and *Commentaries*).

The importance of common grace for the literary enterprise is immense. It means first that we do not need to inquire into the religious orthodoxy of an author before we can affirm what is worthy in an author's work. Wherever we find the true, the good, or the beautiful, we can applaud it. This is far from universally accepted by Christians. Among earnest believers I often sense an uneasiness, if not outright hostility, toward works of literature authored by non-Christians. The doctrine of com-

T. S. Eliot said the following about the need for Christian readers to assess the viewpoints in a work of literature after having analyzed in the ordinary ways: "Literary criticism should be completed by criticism from a definite ethical and theological standpoint. . . . What I believe to be incumbent upon all Christians is the duty of maintaining consciously certain standards and criteria of criticism over and above those applied by the rest of the world; and that by these criteria and standards everything that we read must be tested" ("Religion and Literature").

mon grace leads us to conclude that we can and should spend time reading secular literature as well as Christian literature for our edification and delight.

If we begin with the premise of common grace, we have removed the largest obstacle that we face in reading secular classics. We have not made any prejudgments about whether a given author or text will give us the true, the good, and the beautiful, but we have opened the door to the possibility that this is the case.

This leads to my second proposed method for reading a secular classic: we need to *be open to receive what the work stands ready to offer.* A secular classic is a classic. We can trust that it will present human experience for our contemplation, knowing that such truthfulness to reality is a form of truth that we want in our lives. Second, we can be nearly as certain that a secular classic will give us enjoyment through literary form, technique, verbal skill, and beauty. Third, we know that the work will raise significant issues and embody ideas for us to consider. Even if the interpretive light falls from the wrong angle, the work provides the materials and occasion for us to think and to confirm our understanding of truth.

Another way to state what I have covered in the preceding paragraph is that we should *approach a secular classic with the right expectations.* We should expect to be edified, even though this will not happen in exactly the same way as when we read a Christian classic. We should expect to find human experience clarified and celebrated. We should expect to be entertained. We should expect to be stimulated to think and reach conclusions about ideas that are put before us. It is extremely rare to find a work of literature with which we find nothing to affirm.

Additionally, with secular classics, we need to *be active as Christian readers*. In fact, we need to be extra alert. By definition, a non-Christian work will need to be countered or added to at some points. We need to operate in an awareness of the crucial role that a reader supplies to the process. If an author stops short of expressing a Christian viewpoint, we need to supply the Christian dimension. If an author gets it wrong, we need to correct what has been misrepresented. We are not afforded quite the same luxury of mental and spiritual relaxation as when we read a Christian classic. With some works we need to enter into combat. But there are ways in which this exercise allows us metaphorically to put on muscle in ways that are not true if we read only Christian literature.

Lest I seem to have given too great a vote of confidence to secular classics, let me add the rule: we *need to assimilate a secular work in an awareness of its divergence from our own beliefs.* This divergence is rarely total, but it is always present somewhere. With modern literature, it may be everywhere. We do not need to apologize for avoiding literature that mainly assaults our morality and sensibility, nor for leaving a book unfinished when its liabilities begin to outweigh its value to us.

When we read secular classics, we need to realize that *we can agree with a literary work on some levels without agreeing on all levels.* The reverse of that is also true: *we can disagree with certain aspects of a work without rejecting all aspects of it.* We should be generous when we read a secular classic—not indiscriminate, but generous. We should

"Literature treats, in basic and universal terms, both the affirmations and the problems of human existence. . . . Humane [secular] literature furnishes insight into human life and increases the value of that life by the nurture of beauty, of understanding, and of compassion" (Roland M. Frye, *Perspective on Man*).

expect the best instead of the worst. We are reading a classic, after all, not something cheap and tawdry.

Additionally—and again, perhaps surprisingly—we need to *assume that we can find God in secular literature, even in the literature of unbelief.* We will need to supply a missing element for this to happen, but if we know that this responsibility has fallen to us, we can step to the plate and be edified by secular literature. We can be drawn closer to God through reading it. I remember how turned off I was nearly half a century ago when I read a literary critic who spoke of finding God in the literature of depravity. The context did, indeed, make the position objectionable, since the author fell into the camp of critics (at that point numerous) who apply such a loose definition of Christianity that virtually all literature ends up being "Christian." But the book in question planted a seed in my thinking that has led to the conclusion that we *can*, in fact, find God in literature that does not acknowledge him and may repudiate him. We are supplying something that the work omits. From the same early era of my career came the following statement by British literary scholar Harry Blamires: "There is nothing in our experience, however trivial, worldly, or even evil, which cannot be thought about christianly" (*The Christian Mind*).

"Has [secular literature] any part to play in the life of the converted? I think so, and in two ways. (a) If all the cultural values, on the way up to Christianity, were dim [pointers to] the truth, we can recognize them as such still. And since we must rest and play, where can we do so better than here—in the suburbs of Jerusalem? . . . (b) If . . . cultural activities are innocent and even useful, then they also . . . can be done to the Lord" (C. S. Lewis, *Christian Reflections*).

Chapter Summary

The best way to summarize this chapter is to quote and analyze a key statement in T. S. Eliot's classic essay "Religion and Literature," which deals with the integration of literature and the Christian faith. Here is the statement: "So long as we are conscious of the gulf fixed between ourselves and the greater part of contemporary literature, we are more or less protected from being harmed by it, and are in a position to extract from it what good it has to offer us." We can expand the reference to contemporary literature to include secular literature of whatever type. Eliot's statement is beautifully balanced as it asserts four things about non-Christian literature:

1. There is a gulf between such literature and our Christian convictions.
2. There are potential harms that such literature can inflict on us.
3. The key to not being harmed in this way is to be conscious of the conflict between us and secular authors.
4. And, if we are aware of this, secular literature has much "good . . . to offer us."

CHAPTER 10

Where to Find the Classics

A guide to the classics would be incomplete without a roadmap showing where to find them. Nonetheless, I have composed this chapter with the burden of knowing that anything like a complete list of literary classics is impossible—more so today with the erosion of "the canon" than it would have been three decades ago. Additionally, even if we begin with the premise of a selective list of classics, the venture immediately becomes controversial as valid candidates for inclusion are omitted.

My readers should therefore realize that the books listed in this chapter are not intended as a definitive or complete list. They are a combination of works that I myself have read (and in some cases have taught for nearly half a century) and books that regularly appear on lists of classics or recommended readings. This chapter is no more than a collection of specimens. The works that I name are a good starting point, but I make no claim that a person needs to read all of them or that people should limit their reading to these works.

Lists of classics fall into two categories. The first is the domain of educators who wish to ensure that students are acquainted with the classics required for a competent education. Often such educators wish to design a curriculum composed with an eye on standardized tests or an imagined need for their students to avoid scandal in the eyes of college professors. The second category of lists is designed for self-motivated readers who have completed their formal education and are now in the stage of self-education or enlightened leisure. These readers are lifelong readers. I have an eye on both categories of readers with my list.

Books, Books, Books

In doing the research for this chapter, I found some surprises. For example, there is a whole genre of books *about* books. In fact, there are *bibliographies* of books about books! There are websites that list books about books. These sources typically contain lists of books about books and catchy quotations about the joys of reading.

We all know that there are lists of recommended books and classics.

What I had not realized is *how many* lists are available. Of course, the Internet has greatly expanded their number. The sheer quantity of book lists actually liberated me as I wrote this chapter. The overabundance of lists could easily lead a person to despair of finding a useful list of classics, so the existence of a short list (such as the one represented by this chapter) suddenly seems welcome. Additionally, the variety and disagreement among the lists confirms the point that I am about to make that anyone who is serious about reading the classics needs to assume responsibility for creating a personal list of classics.

In addition to lists of classics, there are numerous sources on the subject of reading. A subgenre is essays and Internet sites on how to find time for reading. I decided not to enter this area because I have nothing to add to existing sources. Many Internet sites yield good ideas that I can enthusiastically endorse.

The lists that I have included in this chapter are literary classics for adult readers, starting with high school. There are many good books and Internet sites about classics of children's literature, a topic that lies beyond my expertise. I have included a few children's books that I consider to also be adult books, along the lines of C. S. Lewis's comment that "a children's story which is enjoyed only by children is a bad children's story. The good ones last" ("On Three Ways of Writing for Children"). I also decided to omit popular literature such as mystery novels.

Creating Your Own List of Classics

With my offenses of omission about to appear, I will put my trump card on the table: every lifelong reader needs to compile a private list of classics. It may or may not resemble the traditional canon of classics, but for us personally, these works meet most or all of the criteria for a classic (the criterion most likely to be missing is cultural influence).

One of the best pieces of advice that I ever encountered in regard to reading came from an old book first published in 1941. To show how much things have changed, the book (*Poetry as a Means of Grace*) was written for ministers by a famous professor of English at Princeton University and was published by Princeton University Press in the United States and Oxford University Press in England. The author, Charles Osgood, wrote the book as a guide and encouragement to preachers to keep up their contact with imaginative literature. In the opening chapter titled "Your Poet," Osgood recommended that even though we should read widely, we should also claim one author as a lifelong specialty. Osgood wrote,

> Whatever else you read, adopt one of the greatest poets as your own for life, one with whom habitual companionship and deepening acquaintance become a more and more abundant source of refreshment and strength, a confirmation of spiritual truth, an elevation to a more comprehensive view of life. Choose this author as friends are chosen, less by deliberate selection than by natural congruence. . . . Read a bit of [this author] as often as you can, until at least parts of him become part of yourself.

I would enlarge the compass of that excellent piece of advice to include the concept of one's own list of classics in addition to a classic author. This was codified for me by an article that appeared in *The American Scholar* ("One Heart's Canon," by Suzanne Rhodenbaugh). While the author's personal canon concentrated on poems, the idea of a personal canon can be applied to classics generally. The author of the article found the academic canon to be of only limited usefulness in determining her own canon, which consists of works that draw her "by some need or connection that is my own." Her summary statement is that the works that reside in her personal canon are the ones that have "offered empowerment and understanding, solace, and livening."

I have gained a new appreciation for the idea of a personal list of classics from some of my publishing projects. When I worked on a jointly authored book entitled *Pastors in the Classics*, I discovered a treasure trove of Christian fiction that I had barely known. Similarly, when I helped to collect poems for inclusion in Kent Hughes's *The Pastor's Book*, I greatly expanded my canon of classic Christian poems. (I have chosen not to include material from the two books I just referenced in my list of classics below, but those two books constitute excellent sources of additional Christian classics.)

As I turn to a beginning list of just *some* classics, I do so with my endorsement of the idea that the list needs to be expanded or shortened, and in any event made personal. Choosing a "life author" is an excellent idea as well. In view of what I have said, I trust that the pressure is off for me to produce a definitive list of classics.

Some Literary Classics

There is no single best way to organize the literary classics. I have mingled chronological considerations, genres, acknowledged "schools" of literature (such as Neoclassical and Romantic), and intellectual allegiance (such as Christian).

Classical (Greco-Roman) Literature

There are three preeminent classical epics—*The Iliad* and *The Odyssey* by the Greek poet Homer and *The Aeneid* by the Roman author Virgil. *The Odyssey* elevates domestic values to supremacy, while the other two are built around martial (military) and political themes. Readers who love *The Odyssey* are unlikely to read the other two epics with as much zest. Additionally, Greek literature is as famous for its dramatic tragedies as its epics. At the top of the list are two tragedies by Sophocles—*Antigone* and *Oedipus Rex*. Some professors of literature would place *Agamemnon* by Aeschylus in the same high category.

Major Christian Classics of the Middle Ages and Renaissance

By way of reminder, I will say that a Christian classic is not simply a work that intersects with the Bible and Christianity but that fully endorses them. Devotional poetry forms a distinct group and is different from the category of major works; I have refrained from listing lyric poems, but of course I do regard many of them as medieval Christian classics. Among masterworks, Dante's *The Divine Comedy* and John Milton's *Paradise Lost* are in a class by themselves. Edmund Spenser's romance *The Faerie Queene* is not quite as explicitly Christian as the previous two, but it belongs in the same elite circle. Milton's closet drama *Samson Agonistes* is in the second tier, as is Augustine's *Confessions* (early medieval), which can be read in a literary manner but is a crossover book that can be read as a religious rather than literary text.

Classics of the Middle Ages

The Middle Ages were dominated by Catholicism, with the result that virtually all medieval classics are to some degree Christian in their allegiance. The towering example is Geoffrey Chaucer's *The Canterbury Tales*. That same author's epic-like poem (technically a romance) *Troilus and Criseyde* is a major classic that is little known today. The Old English epic *Beowulf* is a partly Christian classic. Romances were popular in the Middle Ages, and the best English example is *Sir Gawain the Green Knight*, supplemented by various Arthurian stories ("the matter of Britain," the age called it). The most famous medieval drama is the morality play *Everyman*.

Renaissance Sonnet Cycles

Sonnet cycles were a rage in the sixteenth century; the two greatest ones are Sir Philip Sidney's *Astrophel and Stella* and Shakespeare's *Sonnets*.

Shakespeare's Plays

We can list at least the following Shakespeare plays as "can't miss" classics, since they are all worthy classics: among the comedies, *A Midsummer Night's Dream* and *As You Like It*; among the tragedies (in the order of composition), *Hamlet, Othello, King Lear,* and *Macbeth*; the best last-phase romance is *The Winter's Tale* (an unjustifiably overlooked Christian classic). *The Merchant of Venice* is also a Christian classic if interpreted correctly.

Seventeenth-Century Devotional Poetry

The great era of Christian lyric poetry was the seventeenth century (which is not to deny that poetry of this type has been written in every Christian era, starting with the Bible). The towering figures are John Donne, George Herbert, and John Milton (chiefly his sonnets). The best short religious poems of all three poets appear in *The Devotional Poetry of Donne, Herbert, and Milton*, a volume in the Crossway Guides to the Classics series.

Renaissance Love Poetry

The sixteenth and seventeenth centuries were the greatest era for love poetry in English literature. A good resource for tapping it is an anthology of English literature; the most widely used is *The Norton Anthology of English Literature*. Edmund Spenser's poem "Epithalamion," written for his own wedding, is a Christian classic in the mold of Song of Solomon. Donne's greatest love poems are "A Valediction: Forbidding Mourning," "The Sun Rising," and "The Canonization," but there are excellent second-tier poems as well.

English Neoclassical (Late Seventeenth and Eighteenth Century) Literature

John Dryden, "Ode on the Death of Mrs. Anne Killigrew"; Alexander Pope, "The Rape of the Lock"; Jonathan Swift, *Gulliver's Travels*; Samuel Johnson, *Rasselas*; and John Bunyan, *The Pilgrim's Progress* (possibly the most famous Christian classic beyond the Bible).

Poetry of the Romantic Movement (Nineteenth Century)

When we come to an era in which lyric poetry dominated the literary scene, it becomes difficult to list specific works. Remembering that a classic can be an author as well as a work, I offer the following as a list of classic English and American Romantic poets: William Blake, William Wordsworth, Samuel Taylor Coleridge, Percy Bysshe Shelley, Walt Whitman, and Emily Dickinson. I find it difficult not to start naming favorite poems, but if I start, I would not know where to stop. Anthologies such as *The Norton Anthology of English Literature* and *The Norton Anthology of American Literature* will provide a menu of leading poems by the poets I have named.

Victorian Poetry

The Victorian age in England covered approximately the final two-thirds of the nineteenth century. The major poets were Alfred, Lord Tennyson; Robert Browning; and (less important than those two) Matthew Arnold. Tennyson's major poem is *In Memoriam*. His greatest lyric poem is "Crossing the Bar," but his list of great lyrics is extensive. Browning perfected the genre of the dramatic monologue; the two greatest examples are "Soliloquy of the Spanish Cloister" and "My Last Duchess," but the list could be expanded indefinitely. Matthew Arnold's "Dover Beach" is one of the most frequently anthologized poems in the English language.

Nineteenth-Century English and American Novels

Nathaniel Hawthorne, *The Scarlet Letter*; Herman Melville, *Moby Dick*; Mark Twain, *Huckleberry Finn*; Jane Austen, *Sense and Sensibility, Pride and Prejudice,* and *Emma*; Charles Dickens, *Great Expectations, David Copperfield, Oliver Twist,* and *A Tale of Two Cities*; Charlotte Brontë, *Jane Eyre*; Anthony Trollope, *Barchester Towers*; Thomas Hardy, *The Return of the Native* and *The Mayor of Casterbridge*; and Oscar Wilde, *The Picture of Dorian Gray.* Henry David Thoreau's great Romantic classic, *Walden,* is an autobiography rather than a novel, but worth mentioning here.

Nineteenth-Century Russian Novelists

Fyodor Dostoyevsky, *Crime and Punishment* and *The Brothers Karamazov*; Leo Tolstoy, *War and Peace* and *Anna Karenina.*

Nineteenth-Century Short Stories

Nathaniel Hawthorne, "Young Goodman Brown"; Herman Melville, "Bartleby the Scrivener"; Edgar Allan Poe, "The Tell-Tale Heart" and his other detective and horror stories.

Christian Classics of the Nineteenth Century

Alfred, Lord Tennyson, "Crossing the Bar"; Robert Browning, "Saul"; Gerard Manley Hopkins, numerous devotional poems such as "God's Grandeur," "The Windhover," and "Pied Beauty" (but it would be a shame to stop with those); Francis Thompson, "The Hound of Heaven" and "In No Strange Land" ("O world invisible, we view thee"); Christina Rossetti, "In the Bleak Midwinter" and "Good Friday"; Leo Tolstoy, "The Death of Ivan Ilych" (one of the greatest Christian classics ever).

Modern Novels

The list is endless; I offer the following as the tip of the iceberg: John Steinbeck, *Of Mice and Men, Grapes of Wrath,* and *East of Eden*; Ernest Hemingway, *The Old Man and the Sea* and *The Sun Also Rises*; William Golding, *The Lord of the Flies*; F. Scott Fitzgerald, *The Great Gatsby*; Harper Lee, *To Kill a Mockingbird*; Aldous Huxley, *Brave New World*; Kenneth Grahame, *The Wind in the Willows* (fantasy rather than a novel); and Albert Camus, *The Stranger.*

Christian Classics of the Modern Era

T. S. Eliot, "Journey of the Magi," "The Four Quartets," and *Murder in the Cathedral*; C. S. Lewis, The Chronicles of Narnia, *The Great Divorce*, and *The Screwtape Letters*; J. R. R. Tolkien, The Lord of the Rings. I would also direct you to the numerous works discussed in *Pastors in the Classics* (Baker, 2012).

At this point, seasoned readers will be nearly beside themselves with frustration over my omission of works that they regard as essential. If so, I could not possibly be more pleased, because it proves that they have a personal list of classics. To prompt my readers to possess a personal list of classics is a goal of this book.

I will add the following list of anthologies of Christian poetry. They cast the net more widely than simply classic poems and should be regarded as providing the materials from which a personal list of classic Christian poems can be assembled: *The Story of Jesus in the World's Literature*, ed. Edward Wagenknecht; *Masterpieces of Religious Verse*, ed. James Dalton Morrison; *The Country of the Risen King: An Anthology of Christian Poetry*, ed. Merle Meeter; *A Sacrifice of Praise: An Anthology of Christian Poetry in English*, ed. James H. Trott.

Reflections on Reading

A book on the classics is by its very nature a book about reading. People who love the classics are readers. I will therefore conclude with some favorite quotations about books and reading.

"Some books are to be tasted, others to be swallowed, and some few [i.e., the classics] to be chewed and digested."

Francis Bacon
"Of Studies"

"It is a good rule, after reading a new book, never to allow yourself another new one till you have read an old one in between. If that is too much for you, you should at least read one old one to every three new ones."

C. S. Lewis
"On the Reading of Old Books"

Lewis claimed that "clearly one must read every good book at least once every ten years."

C. S. Lewis
The Letters of C. S. Lewis to Arthur Greeves (1914–1963)

"There are worse crimes than burning books. One of them is not reading them."

Joseph Brodsky
"New Poet Laureate Meets the Press"

"A great book should leave you with many experiences, and slightly exhausted at the end. You live several lives while reading [it]."

William Styron
Conversations with William Styron

"What you don't read is often as important as what you do read."

Lemony Snicket
The Vile Village

"We read books to find out who we are. What other people, real or imaginary, do and think and feel . . . is an essential guide to our understanding of what we ourselves are and may become."

Ursula Le Guin
The Language of the Night

"A classic is a book that has never finished saying what it has to say."

Italo Calvino
The Uses of Literature

"Children are made readers on the laps of their parents."

Emilie Buchwald
source unknown

"We read to know we are not alone."

C. S. Lewis
Shadowlands

"That [we are not alone] is part of the beauty of all literature. You discover that your longings are universal longings, that you're not lonely and isolated from anyone. You belong."

F. Scott Fitzgerald as remembered by
Sheilah Graham in *The Beloved Infidel*

"One of our most ordinary reactions to a good piece of literary art is expressed in the formula, 'This is what I always felt and thought, but have never been able to put clearly into words, even for myself.'"

Aldous Huxley
"Tragedy and the Whole Truth"

"Why are we reading, if not in the hope of beauty laid bare, life heightened and its deepest mystery probed?"

Annie Dillard
The Writing Life

"I love reading another reader's list of favorites. Even when I find I do not share their tastes or predilections, I am provoked to compare, contrast, and contradict."

T. S. Eliot
source unknown

"All books are divisible into two classes, the books of the hour, and the books of all time. . . . There are good books for the hour, and good books for all time; bad books for the hour, and bad books for all time."

John Ruskin
Sesame and Lilies

"What is it that separate reading acts share [beyond] the setting, characters, and narrative particulars of any given book? . . . I study people in the aisles of bookstores, . . . standing in place with their necks tilted at a 45-degree angle, looking not for a specific book, but for a book they can trust to do the job. They want plot and character, sure, but what they really want is a vehicle that will bear them off to the reading state. . . . If anything has changed about my reading over the years, it is that I value the state a book puts me in more than I value the specific contents."

Sven Birkerts
"The Woman in the Garden"

"In reading a book which is an old favorite with me . . . I not only have the pleasure of imagination and of a critical relish of the work, but the pleasures of memory added to it. . . . [Old books] are landmarks and guides in our journey through life."

William Hazlitt
"On Reading Old Books"

"It's a good idea to have your own books with you in a strange place."

Cornelia Funke
Inkheart

In answer to the question, How should Christians write and read literature? "For the glory of God and for fun."

Kay Baxter
Conference address at Wheaton College

Printed in Great Britain
by Amazon

55166585R00064